Rags and Patches

Rags and Patches

Bill Maddox and Harold Beeson

Jacket Painting by
Franz Altschuler

 Follett Publishing Company/ Chicago

Library of Congress Cataloging in Publication Data:

Maddox, Bill, 1938-
    Rags and Patches.

    SUMMARY: Relates the adventures of 13-year-old Danny Ragsdale and his dog Patches as they search for Danny's father in south Texas.
    [1. Adventure stories. 2. Dogs—Fiction]
I. Beeson, Harold, 1939-   joint author.
II. Altschuler, Franz. III. Title.
PZ7.M2559Rag [Fic] 78-3218

International Standard Book Number: 0-695-80966-0 Trade Binding
International Standard Book Number: 0-695-40966-2 Library Binding

Second Printing

Thanks
to Sheila, Rhonda and Mariah Beeson, for
    their encouragement and understanding;
to Mary Jane, Amy and Stacy Maddox,
    for the pure joy they bring;
to Jim deNeve, whose dream of Rags
    and Patches is now reality;
to Lloyd Hayes, who helped Jim deNeve
    and others realize their dreams;
and, to those remarkable Cajuns of Texas
    and Louisiana, who were the real
    inspiration for this story.

1

A SUDDEN GUST of summer wind caused hundreds of little waves to dance on the surface of the bayou and sent the nose of the pirogue veering into the cypress knees standing like sentinels along the bank.

Danny Ragsdale plunged the long pole into the tea-colored water and, with strong brown arms straining, sent the narrow craft back out into the sunlit middle of the stream. The thirteen-year-old knew the low, thick branches shading the edge of the bayou were favorite resting places for water moccasins. Danny remembered all the stories he had heard concerning hunters or fishermen suddenly abandoning their boat upon finding a snake crawling around in it.

Tossing his head to clear the long, auburn hair from his eyes, the boy seemed to be a part of the slender shell of the boat as it glided across the sun-flecked water. His supple body was covered only by an extremely ragged pair of bib overalls.

He had recently wondered more than once if maybe his clothing—not his name Ragsdale—had earned him his nickname "Rags" from the other students at Cow Bayou School.

It wasn't that the other kids were unfriendly; only that Rags had been what his mother had called a loner. After she had died nearly three months earlier, he had become even more remote, his spirit remaining in the wild vastness of the swamp even while he was in the classroom.

He thought of his mother now as he guided the pirogue along the bayou. Emmaline Boudreaux Ragsdale. Rags' father called her Em. Rags would not have been wearing ragged clothes to school had she still been alive.

For as long as Rags could remember knowing her, his mother had been the center of the family, motivating the joys of the three Ragsdales and soothing the infrequent pains.

She seemed always to be there when needed. Rags had innocently felt she was immortal; that she would always be available.

Mrs. Ragsdale was of Acadian descent. Acadian, she had explained to her son, was the name given the hardy Frenchmen who originally immigrated to Canada and resided in the colony of Acadia. Later, uprooted by the British, they left that northern region to settle along the coast of Louisiana. Acadian evolved to "Cajun," Rags' mother told him. "Nothing better than a good Cajun," Rags' father would tease.

Emmaline Boudreaux Ragsdale had been an only child, as was Rags' father. When Rags in earlier years had wondered aloud why he was the only child, his mother had delicately dismissed the subject by telling him, "There's just too much love wrapped up in you, *mon cher.*" Then she had added, "Your father and I have perfection in one. We've been blessed enough."

Rags, poling the pirogue, pictured her standing in the door of the Ragsdale house, her hands folded into an apron, bidding farewell to Rags and his father as they left for one of their frequent hunting or fishing trips into the southeast Texas swamp.

While Rags' father had provided the boy an opportunity to grow in love and respect for the marsh country, it was his mother who introduced him to the ways of religion, sacrifice, respect for others, gentleness combined with courage, and admiration for life.

Life, Rags thought. Life had gone from this tender, forgiving woman in late February, just at the arrival of her favorite season, Lenten, those forty days leading to Easter Sunday.

One Saturday morning she had been there, smiling with her husband as Rags set out alone to fish far downstream in the bayou.

That afternoon, when Rags returned, she was dead—the victim of an automobile accident in which her husband had been the driver.

Rags' father had not been himself after that. He was seldom home. Rags' loneliness had slowly evaporated in the tangles and immenseness of the swamp.

Rags' reverie was suddenly broken by a sound so faint he could not at first identify it. Years of experience in the swamp, however, told him something was not as it should be.

The boy drove the pirogue under the hanging branches, into the shore, and grasped a tall cypress knee. He cupped his hand behind his ear and waited for the wind to die down. The sound filtered through the moss-draped trees again, and this time Rags thought he recognized it as the terrified yelping of a puppy.

He leaped to the bank and pulled the little boat after him. Moving slowly at first, then faster as the direction of shrill barking became apparent, his toughened bare feet carried him across fallen logs and through the shallow water of the swamp.

As swiftly as the boy moved, his mind raced even faster. "It must be Devil's Sinkhole," he told himself, "where I saw that fox go under the quicksand last year."

Seconds later Rags plunged from a thicket into a small clearing. He immediately realized he had been only half right. There were two young dogs struggling to stay atop the surface of the treacherous muck. It was obvious that in the next minute or so the deadly hole would claim two more victims.

"Not if I can help it," he vowed between clenched teeth as he sprinted toward a slender water oak hanging over the bed of quicksand. Without breaking stride, he leaped into the lower branches of the tree and began pulling himself to the top.

As the trunk narrowed, Rags could feel his

weight begin to bend the tree toward the young dogs, whose shrill cries had increased as their efforts to remain above the surface became more feeble.

Ever so slowly the water oak descended toward the desperate pups. The boy inched outward until his legs were wrapped around a section of the trunk no larger than his wrist. Swaying perilously over the deadly trap, he let his torso drop and reached for the nearest dog. Once, twice, his fingers grazed the shoulder of the struggling puppy. Suddenly his hand closed around one of the soft ears. Rags jerked the yelping young animal to his chest before grasping the trunk with his left hand and pulling his body to a horizontal position. Like the shot-putters he had seen at the high school track meet, he drove the puppy through the air toward the bank. It landed in a clump of reeds and lay there, whimpering.

The boy turned his head carefully and looked for the other young dog. It was gone. Without wasting time on remorse, Rags began inching along the trunk toward the bank. He knew the tree had already held longer than he had any right to expect.

Once over firm ground, Rags released his hold on the trunk and fell into a cushion of leaf mold. He lay there for several minutes, breathing heavily and waiting for the trembling in his exhausted arms to stop. Finally, he rose and looked for the puppy. It was there where he had tossed it, peering fearfully at him through two big, brown eyes.

As he moved toward the dog, it stood unsteadily to its feet and began backing toward the quicksand. Rags stopped, remembering what Uncle Wash had told him about approaching strange dogs.

"If you jes' walks up to a dog what don't know you," the old black man had explained, "and stand 'way up there over him, he's gonna think you tryin' to hurts him."

Rags thought of the big, gentle hands that were equally at home caring for a sick animal or playing a fiddle and wished Uncle Wash was with him now. The puppy looked ready to dash out into the quicksand again.

"You gots to git yo' eyes jes' about level with his," Uncle Wash had continued, "dat way, he won't be so scared."

Rags dropped to his knees and began talking softly to the young dog. The puppy watched him intently, poised for flight. The boy continued to croon, clapping his hands together lightly. There was a slight sideways movement of the pup's tail, then two more.

Rags moved on his knees toward the frightened animal until he was able to reach out and stroke the muddy, yellow fur. He gathered the puppy into his arms and, still stroking him and talking gently, began to walk toward the pirogue.

By the time the pair reached Rags' camp on the edge of the swamp, it was plain the puppy had accepted the boy as a friend. He had rested quietly in the front of the pirogue, his eyes never leaving his rescuer.

The narrow boat glided among the huge cypress trees and came to rest against the sloping bank of a small hummock that rose some three feet above the placid backwater of the bayou. Rags had chosen the spot for his camp because only in the worst weather was the elevated land under water.

The camp itself was a crude lean-to built of material Rags had scavenged from abandoned fishing camps along the bayou. Covered with two layers of corrugated iron and daubed with tar, the roof of the structure did a fairly good job of keeping out the frequent rains that swept the marshy country. It did a much better job, Rags had reflected more than once, than did the patched up wire screen on the sides of the camp in keeping out the hungry, ever-present mosquitoes.

The boy, who had always wanted a dog, remembered something else Uncle Wash had told him about gaining the trust of an animal.

"A dog ain't no peoples," the old man had said. "He ain't gonna love you 'cause you purty or 'cause you gots a personality. He gonna love you 'cause you good to him and 'cause you make him mind you. . . . The best way to be good to him is to feed him when he's hungry. Ain't never seen a dog dat didn't 'preciate dat."

"I bet you are hungry," Rags said to his new-found friend. The dog's tail thumped against the leafy ground in agreement.

The boy quickly built a fire under a hanging pot, then rummaged through a nearby covered box.

"We ain't got but three eggs left," he told the puppy, which followed him closely as he moved about the camp.

He walked to the water's edge, felt momentarily under the dark surface and brought out a line with a big blue catfish on it. "But we ain't gonna go hungry as long as there's fish in this swamp," he said, holding it above his head. The young dog barked at the flouncing blue cat.

Several minutes later, Rags was pulling bits of fish from the bone and feeding them to the puppy, who gulped them down eagerly.

As the pair finished their meal, the boy began talking to the dog. "Tomorrow we'll go by Uncle Wash's house and get us some of that good ol' milk. You'll like him. He knows all about dogs.

"But before we go, you're gonna have to be washed up. You can't go looking all muddy."

Rags carried the dog to the edge of the bayou and began bathing his mud-caked body. As the dirt was rinsed away, Rags noticed bare spots in the dog's yellow fur. "How'd you get these scrapes on you, boy?" Rags asked. "You've got fur missing all over."

Later, as Rags rested against a tree, the puppy laid his head across the boy's outstretched ankle and gazed up at him. "After we go to Uncle Wash's tomorrow, we'll go by my pa's house and get us some eggs," the youngster said.

"But," he sternly warned the dog, "you got to behave yourself and leave his chickens alone."

The puppy's pink tongue ran out once and licked the hand that moved to rub his head. Worn out from the day's exertion and soothed by a good meal and the knowledge that he had a friend, the young dog went to sleep.

Rags continued to stroke the yellow fur. He was too excited to sleep. At last, he had a dog.

2

THE PINK, ORANGE, AND YELLOW STREAKS of first sunlight had already given way to the brassy, still heat of a southeastern Texas late spring morning when Rags tied his boat and began trotting up the well-worn path to Uncle Wash's cabin. The dog followed at Rags' heels.

A few minutes later the two emerged into a clearing, in the middle of which sat a small, neat, unpainted cabin surrounded by a picket fence. From the rear of the cabin came the bleating of a goat.

"That's Veronica," Rags informed the dog. "Uncle Wash says she's a better watch dog than Bernis."

As if he had heard his name, a large black dog bounded from the cabin and came to meet the newly arrived pair. After sniffing the younger dog, the black animal allowed Rags to scratch behind his ears.

"I thought Veronica was tellin' me somebody was here."

Rags looked up to see an old black man with a cane moving slowly around the corner of the cabin.

"Hi, Uncle Wash," the boy shouted. "Look what I got," he said, holding the puppy up for inspection.

"Well, I do declare," the old man exclaimed. He took the dog from the boy and examined it closely. "He a fine dog. Little skinny, maybe. Must weigh 'bout twenty pounds. It maybe three or four months old. I do believe he may be part Labrador, like Bernis here. Prob'ly make you a good duck dog."

Uncle Wash felt the dog's exposed skin where fur was missing. The old man raised his eyebrows.

"What do you think happened, Uncle Wash?" Rags inquired.

"Boy," Uncle Wash frowned, "these do look like bad scrapes from somethin'. Look like where he maybe hit the gravel. I do declare this youngun' may've been throwed out a car. Where'd he come from?" Uncle Wash handed the dog back to Rags, who placed him on the ground.

Rags described the events of the day before, explaining how he had been unable to save one puppy.

"Fed him yet?" Uncle Wash asked the boy.

"Yes, sir. Remembered what you told me about making friends with a dog," Rags proudly said. "Fed him some fresh fish."

"That's good. Mighty good," said Uncle Wash, putting a gnarled hand to Rags' head.

Uncle Wash chuckled. "I sho' am gettin' hungry myself. How 'bout you?" he asked the boy.

Rags hesitated a moment. "Well, I guess I could eat something."

Inside the cabin Uncle Wash filled a pan with bacon and placed it on the wood stove.

"How yo' daddy doin'?" he asked.

"All right, I guess."

"How long it been since you seen him?"

Rags turned and examined the pictures on the wall, most of them outdoor scenes clipped from magazines.

"I dunno," he finally answered. "Last week, I reckon."

Uncle Wash turned the sizzling bacon in the skillet. "He sho' changed since yo' mama passed on. He still hang 'round wi' dat Lewt Wilson?"

"I guess so."

"Dat Wilson," Uncle Wash fumed. "He's the worse thing evuh to come outta dat Jericho commun'ty. Nuthin' but a bunch o' gamblers 'n cockfighters come outta der."

"That's what Momma always said," Rags agreed.

"Ain't nothin' wrong with cockfightin', you unnerstan'. I used to do it myself before I got too old. But all dat drinkin' and gamblin', it jes' ain't no good for a man."

He raked the browned bacon out of the pan and dropped a couple of eggs into the grease. "I remember when he was jes' about your age. Jes' like you. Couldn't keep him outta dat swamp. Sometimes me and him would stay out der for weeks, jes' trappin' and fishin'."

The two ate in silence for several minutes. Finally Uncle Wash turned and took an old fiddle and a bow down from the wall.

"Wipe yo' hands and take this," the old man said. "You ain't been comin' 'round here and practicin' like I tole you to."

Rags ran his palms down the legs of his overalls and took the instrument. Setting it under his chin, he hit a few random notes, then broke into a lively tune.

The melody was suddenly interrupted by Uncle Wash's loud boom of laughter. "Would you look at dat?" he exclaimed. The young dog, who had followed Rags into the cabin, was standing on his hind legs and moving about as if dancing.

"You all right, little patched-up dog," the old man said delightedly.

The music stopped suddenly. "By golly, that's it," Rags shouted to the dog. "You're a pitiful looking patch and your name is Patches."

"I think dat a fittin' name, Patches. Dat do jes' fine," Uncle Wash observed.

The boy played several more tunes and during each one the young dog rose on his hind legs and seemed to waltz around the floor of the cabin.

"Ain't never seen nothin' like it," Uncle Wash said. "He ought to be in a circus or somethin'."

Rags placed the fiddle and bow back on the wall peg. "Well, I guess I better be going."

"Where you goin'? You don't need to go noplace."

"I'm gonna go by the house and get some eggs. You told me once eggs were good for a dog's coat.

Pa ain't there enough to eat many anyway. I'll bring you some back."

The old man shrugged. "Why don't you leave this little Patches dog with me? I'll get some sulphur and oil to put on those spots. Besides, you don't want him 'round those chickens of yo' daddy's anyway."

"Aw, he wouldn't chase 'em," Rags protested.

"Don't you be too sure. 'Less he's trained, a dog's gonna do what his blood tells him to do. This here's a bird dog. It's just natural for him to wants to catch a bird."

Uncle Wash reached down and picked up the yellow puppy. "I believe I even got an old collar 'round here. I'll punch some holes in it and make it fit this patched-up dog."

Rags was out the door and through the fence before Patches realized he was going. As he turned down the path leading to his father's house, the boy could hear the puppy howling after him. A few minutes later, deep into the woods, the trees blocked out the sound. Rags began to run.

A quarter of an hour later, Rags stopped at the edge of a clearing and surveyed his father's home. What had once been a neat, white picket fence now showed signs of disrepair, the gate hanging open on one hinge.

Weeds had taken over the flowerbeds, and the grass was knee-high except for that part of the yard where some two dozen roosters strutted proudly and crowed their defiance to each other. Their combativeness was thwarted by a stout cord tied to a leg of each one and securely staked to the ground.

An unlatched screen door opened and slammed fitfully shut with each gust of spring wind.

"Pa?" Rags called into the open door.

There was no answer. It was obvious that the house was empty.

The boy slipped inside, pausing only momentarily to glance at the dusty photograph of a man, woman, and baby that hung on the wall.

He was back outside in a few minutes, carrying a small bundle of clothes. He entered the hen house and quickly filled a tied-up shirt with the small eggs.

Before he left, Rags filled the feeders with grain and strewed a liberal amount around the roosters' area. After carrying water from the backyard pump to the chickens, he picked up his small bundle and disappeared into the woods.

Back at Uncle Wash's cabin, Patches sported his new collar and a fresh coat of sulphur and oil. He showed his joy at Rags' return by leaping in the air and yelping excitedly.

"I got to go over to ole Miss Luker's house and tend to the garden," Uncle Wash told the boy. "You welcome to stay. I'll be back later."

Rags refused the offer but did accept the jar of sulphur and oil the old man had prepared to heal Patches' scrapes. After filling a jug with drinking water, he and the dog made their way back to the pirogue and, a few minutes later, were on the water again.

On the way back to the camp, Rags stopped long enough to run his "trotlines." This was a series of hooks and lines tied to a heavier cord which was stretched from one side of the bayou to the other. Baited with small fish, trotlines were a favorite method of catching catfish in the bayou country.

Using a hook fashioned from a nail driven into the end of a pole and bent, the boy found his lines and brought them to the surface. Pulling hand-over-hand along the heavy cord, he propelled the boat through the water while checking his catch.

Rags' first trotline yielded three blue catfish, each about a foot long.

"Well, that's enough for our supper tonight," he told the dog. Patches barked as the fish flopped in the bottom of the pirogue.

Rags poled the narrow craft into the current and floated downstream to where his other line ran from a cypress knee along the bank to a sunken log in the middle of the stream.

He found the line with the aid of his homemade hook and raised it to the surface. Grasping the cord with his hand, Rags froze as he felt something—something very big—pull against his line.

Kneeling in the bottom of the pirogue, the boy pulled the boat toward something threshing in the water. A gray-green mottled back appeared, then jerked the line from the boy's hand as it dove once again to the murky depths of the bayou.

Rags recognized it immediately as being a flathead catfish or, as the local folks called them, an Opelousas. The Op in the water appeared to the boy to be as long as he was, probably a fifty-pounder or more, although he knew a fish always looked bigger out of the boat than in.

He knew he could never manage to pull the big fish into the boat alone. He thought of Uncle Wash, then realized the old man's stiffened fingers would handicap any effort he might make at landing the Op and remembered that, anyway, Uncle Wash had gone to the Luker place earlier that morning.

There was his father, of course. But where was his father? He would be the logical person to help Rags, since he had taught him almost all he knew about the swamp. He wouldn't know where to begin looking for the elder Ragsdale, however, and the big fish sure wasn't going to stay on the line forever.

"It looks like it's just me and you, Patches," he told the dog.

Patches whined in eagerness to help his master.

Rags decided on a plan of action. He poled out to the sunken log and untied the end of the line. A few pushes on the long pole put the pirogue back on the bank.

He tied the loose end of the trotline to a tree several feet in from the edge of the water and then, ever so carefully, began to pull the big fish toward the shore.

The big Opelousas came in easily until it reached the shallow water a few feet off the bank. Its body arched once in the air and came down with a splash. Immediately Rags was on top of him, his muscled arms wrapped around the big fish's middle.

Over and over they rolled about in the shallow water. Rags felt the fish slipping from his grasp, then suddenly regained his hold as Patches charged into the water and clamped his teeth onto the tail of the big Op. The boy and the dog rolled the fish onto the bank, where Rags took a stout piece of cord from his pocket, ran it through the Opelousas' gills and fastened the line to a limb overhead.

After shoving the fish back into the water, the boy sat down to catch his breath. Patches came up and licked his cheek.

He grabbed the dog around the neck and held him tightly.

"You're the best fish dog there ever was," he whispered fiercely. "That Op is a good four feet long and must weigh fifty pounds."

Patches wagged his tail and barked loudly. He was evidently feeling very proud of himself.

3

THE NEXT MONTH was a time of learning and growing for both the boy and the dog. They grew in knowledge of each other and of the swamp that had become their home. Patches, on a steady diet of fish, small game, and occasional eggs taken from the Ragsdale home, gained weight rapidly and lost the patches that had given him his name.

The boy's physical growth was not as obvious as the dog's, but his growing independence from civilization was obvious to Uncle Wash. The old man was disturbed that Rags' appearances had become less and less frequent.

The visits were always the same. First there was a meal, then the boy would play several tunes on the fiddle which the old man's arthritic fingers could no longer handle.

After the music, the boy would leave Patches

tied at Uncle Wash's cabin while he raced through the woods to his father's house and gathered a shirt-ful of eggs. Then it was back to the old man's home for the dog and a return to the swamp.

The pattern of Rags and Patches' lives was broken early one sultry morning, however. The two had shoved off in the pirogue just after daylight to check the trotlines. Not having taken a single fish on one of his lines for three days, the boy decided to move it to another location.

Noticing a likely spot, he tied one end of the line to a submerged log in the middle of the bayou and poled the pirogue toward a section of the bank where erosion had worn the earth away and left a mazelike pattern of roots running down into the water.

Rags selected one of the larger roots and leaned forward to tie the end of the line around it. As he did, Patches gave a warning growl and leaped forward onto Rags' arm.

"What . . ." Rags shouted at the dog before he saw the long, gray form attached to Patches' shoulder.

He recoiled in horror as the cold, damp body of the snake passed across his hand. Then Patches had the moccasin between his teeth, shaking it savagely back and forth in a fury. With a final toss of his head, he flung the reptile into the water.

Rags pulled his dog onto his lap and parted the short, yellow fur on Patches' shoulder. Two tiny red punctures showed high on his right foreleg.

Quickly removing the pocketknife his father

had given him for his birthday two years before, the boy made a tiny slit above one of the holes. With a growl, Patches' teeth closed down on his wrist, not enough to break the skin, but enough to give a clear warning.

Still holding the dog closely, Rags began to stroke his head.

"Easy now, easy," he crooned softly. "You know I'm not going to hurt you any more than I have to. I gotta do this, Patches, I got to."

The dog, seemingly satisfied, dropped his head back in the boy's lap. Rags quickly made an incision over the other puncture and placed his lips over the wounds. He drew a small amount of blood from the cuts and spat it over the side of the boat. Eight more times he repeated the process before he was satisfied he had removed as much of the venom as he could.

Wrapping Patches' leg with an old cloth he used for a handkerchief, Rags placed the dog gently in the bottom of the boat and took up the pole. He knew Patches' best chance for life lay in the healing hands of Uncle Wash.

Later Rags would remember very little of their flight across the swamp. The vivid impressions swam together, a memory of limbs and vines tearing at his face as he took the shortest route to the old man's cabin, a memory of leaden arms and a searing pain in his chest as again and again and again he pushed the long pole into the murky water of the swamp, and, worst, the heart-stopping fear as the pole once stuck in the mud and almost tore loose from his grip.

At last the pirogue nosed onto the bank at

Uncle Wash's landing. Patches struggled to rise. The boy scooped him up into his arms.

"Now you lie easy," he told him. "You can't make the blood circulate any faster."

During his stay in the swamp, Patches had grown to more than forty pounds weight. The boy's bare feet landed on the bank. He stumbled once, then lurched up the path, the dog pressed against his chest.

Every step was an effort that tore the breath from his lungs in whistling gasps. Never had the familiar trail seemed so long. The well-known landmarks of trees and bushes and clearings seemed to recede before his blurred vision.

Finally he made the last turn in the path that led to Uncle Wash's clearing. Stumbling through the picket gate, he stood swaying before the cabin.

"Uncle Wash!" he croaked, his voice little more than a whisper. There was no sign of life from the cabin. He looked down at Patches. The dog's eyes drooped, and he seemed to be going to sleep.

The boy slumped to his knees, unable to support Patches' weight any longer. The dog rolled from his arms and lay on the ground, uninterested in his surroundings.

"Please . . . please," the boy sobbed.

He drew a deep breath. "Uncle Wash!" he screamed.

Bernis loped around the corner of the cabin and headed straight for the pair. Nosing aside the bloody rag that covered Patches' leg, he began licking the wound.

Suddenly the old man was there, breathing heavily. His stiffened fingers closed on the boy's arms and pulled him to his feet.

"What happened?" he shouted into Rags' tear-stained face.

The boy tried to answer, but the sobs choked back the words. "Snake . . . snake," was all he could manage to blurt out.

Uncle Wash stooped and lifted the dog as if he were a stuffed toy. Ignoring his cane where it had fallen, he limped toward the cabin and laid Patches on a shady part of the porch.

"Bring me my cane," he ordered the boy.

Rags handed him the stick, and the old man disappeared around the corner of the cabin. The boy sat on the porch and began to softly stroke the dog's head. The leg the snake had struck was already beginning to swell.

Rags never knew how long Uncle Wash was gone. It could have been minutes or almost an hour. Suddenly the old man was there, limping past him up the cabin steps without a word. He returned a few minutes later with a steaming pot in his hand. Using a fork, he dipped a green mass of leaves from the hot water and placed it on the wound. Patches whined as the steaming poultice touched the open cuts.

"Dat's all right," Uncle Wash said soothingly. "We gonna draw dat poison right outta der." He quickly bound the leaves to the dog's leg with a clean, soft cloth.

"Now," he said, turning to the boy, "you go

'round to the pump and wash yo' face."

When Rags returned the old man brought out a bottle of Merthiolate and painted the scratches caused by the wild flight through the swamp. As Uncle Wash daubed the red antiseptic onto his face, the boy told him about the trotline and the snake and how Patches had taken the venom intended for him.

"Is he gonna be all right?" Rags asked the old man. He tried to stop the tears from welling up in his eyes.

"De Lawd knows what dat pup did. He won't let nothin' bad happen to him, you can bet on dat."

The hot summer sun rose to midday and began its descent toward evening. Rags maintained his vigil beside the dog, refusing Uncle Wash's call to eat and leaving the porch only once to bring water, which the dog ignored.

As the evening shadows lengthened across the clearing in front of the cabin, the old man limped onto the porch and stood beside the boy.

"Here," he said, pressing a bacon sandwich into the boy's hand, "you eat this. It ain't gonna do him no good for you to go hungry."

Rags bit into the meat and bread, but he had no appetite with Patches lying beside him near death.

Uncle Wash spread a quilt beside the dog. "I know you ain't gonna come inside so you jes' go ahead and lay out here tonight."

Rags placed the sandwich on the porch and crawled onto the quilt. Although his body was tired and sore, he knew he could not sleep that night. His mind still tumbled with the scenes of the morning.

Yet a few minutes later, he lay snoring softly beside his dog.

A strange sound woke Rags just at daylight next morning. At first he could not remember where he was. Then, just as the memory of the terrible thing that had happened returned, he heard the sound again.

Raising up on one elbow, he looked around and leaped to his feet with a happy shout. Patches had crawled over to the discarded sandwich and was busily crunching the bacon.

Rags' yells brought Uncle Wash onto the porch still pulling on his clothing.

The old man's face broke into a happy grin when he realized the reason for Rags' shouts. "I tole you he wuz gonna be all right, didn't I?"

The boy was unable to answer. He knelt beside Patches and held him as tightly as he could without squeezing the wounded leg. His dog was going to live.

4

It was easy for Uncle Wash to persuade Rags to stay with him while Patches recovered from the snakebite. The boy knew his dog needed rest, and he felt confident the old man would know what to do in case there was a turn for the worse.

Each morning Uncle Wash would leave for the widow Luker's home, where he worked as a handyman and gardener. During his absence Rags would shove off alone in the pirogue and, more often than not, have a mess of fish cleaned and ready for the frying pan when the old man returned in the afternoon. Fish, Uncle Wash had often said, were something he "ain't never ate too much of."

In the evening, Uncle Wash always saw to it that Rags practiced on the fiddle.

As Rags pushed away from the bank each morning, it became more and more difficult to leave

Patches behind. The rapidly recovering dog would follow the boy to the water's edge and whine pitifully as the pirogue disappeared into the swamp. As much as Rags wanted his dog's company, however, he knew that rest was the best medicine for Patches' recovery.

On the fifth day of their stay in the cabin, Rags decided to return to his father's house for some more eggs. He knew the nourishment they provided would help restore Patches' strength.

As he crossed the clearing in front of the cabin, Rags heard a sound behind him. It was Patches.

"No!" he said sternly. "You gotta stay here."

The dog whined and looked pleadingly at the boy.

"I know you're strong enough to go, but Uncle Wash says you shouldn't be around those chickens. Now go on back."

Patches hesitated, then turned and walked back toward the cabin, a picture of dejection with his tail between his legs and his head almost touching the ground.

Rags jogged down the familiar trail toward his father's home. As he neared the house, his steps slowed and a feeling of disquiet came over him. It was the same sense of uneasiness he felt each time he returned to the house where he had been born and raised.

The memory of his mother was still there, but it was as if it had been cloaked with something not quite clean, something he disliked and wanted to strike out against and didn't know how.

As Rags emerged from the woods, he realized

the place was not empty. Parked in front were several pickup trucks and a couple of cars. From the backyard came the sound of voices and occasional laughter.

As he turned the corner of the house, Rags saw two dozen or more men grouped loosely in a circle. In the center two red and black roosters flew at each other, then fell back.

"Hey, son!" exclaimed a stocky, red-haired man breaking away from the crowd and walking unevenly toward Rags.

"Hello, Pa," Rags said. The smell of whiskey caused him to turn his head as the man placed an arm around his neck and held him close.

"Where you been, boy?" the older Ragsdale asked, his pale blue eyes slightly out of focus.

"I been staying with Uncle Wash, Pa."

"That's good, son, that's good." He patted the boy clumsily on the shoulder.

"Hey, Red! You owe me ten," shouted a slim, dark man leaning against a pickup truck. He took a long drink from a flat bottle and returned it to a side pocket of his frayed black suit coat. He passed the back of his hand across his lips and then wiped the moisture on his faded blue jeans. Carefully avoiding a mud puddle, his gleaming white sneakers carried him toward the Ragsdales. A battered straw hat shaded his cold, expressionless eyes.

Behind him the crowd had broken apart slightly to let the handler of the victorious cock carry his bloody charge to his cage. Two more roosters were being brought into the ring.

The elder Ragsdale pulled a small wad of bills

from his pocket. He counted out nine one-dollar bills, then added some change to the pile in the dark man's hand.

"There it is, Lewt, you son-of-a-gun. You broke me today."

The other man laughed, exposing one long, yellow tooth in the front of his mouth. Under several days' growth of beard, his pale skin looked unhealthy in the morning sunlight.

"So this is yer little swamp critter, eh?" he asked, nodding at Rags.

"Say hello to Mister Wilson, son."

Rags mumbled a greeting and turned his head. He had never liked Lewt Wilson. He could remember his mother's contempt for the man she called "the snake." The cold, hooded yellow eyes and the one long, fanglike tooth did remind Rags of a snake, although the boy knew it was not Wilson's appearance that prompted his mother to give him the name.

Now here he was, leaning arrogantly against the house that had been her pride and taking money from Rags' father. The boy felt anger welling up inside.

"Y'all ain't gonna bet on Rocky's rooster?" asked a short, wiry, middle-aged man who had just joined the group. He removed a bottle from the back pocket of his faded overalls and took a long drink. Replacing the whiskey, he ran his fingers through the colorless fringe of hair that circled the red, peeling skin on top of his head.

He prompted Wilson: "You'd better bet on Rocky's rooster."

Lewt seemed uninterested.

"That's the cock that won the derby over in Louisiana," the short man added.

Wilson held out the money Rags' father had just given him. "Here, see how much you can get me for this, Shorty."

Shorty took the money and turned away. He stopped and looked at Rags. "This'n must belong to you, Red," he said, nodding at the boy.

"Where you been living, boy?" Wilson asked suddenly.

Rags looked at him intently, determined to neither answer nor look away first. It was none of Wilson's business where he had been living.

"He's been staying with Uncle Wash," the boy's father answered.

"Wash?" Wilson asked in surprise. "Well, I'll be. Here you got a good place, and he's over there staying with an old . . ."

Wilson's observations were suddenly interrupted by a loud squawk and a series of barks from the other side of the house. With a sinking feeling, Rags ran toward the noise.

As he turned the corner, a dozen or more hens erupted from the chicken house with an excited yellow dog in hot pursuit.

"Patches!" Rags yelled.

The boy's voice was lost in the uproar from the screaming chickens, the barking dog, and the shouts of the cockfight audience as the hen house emptied at them like a scatter gun.

One obviously intoxicated man drew back and aimed a kick at Patches, which missed by at least three feet. The man sat down with the other leg crumpled under him.

Rags made a dive for Patches and missed. As he raised himself from the dust, a chill ran through him. Wilson had grabbed a shotgun from one of the pickup trucks and was trying to get a clear shot at Patches.

"No!" the boy shouted, and leaped toward the tall men with the gun.

The shotgun roared and Rags heard Patches give a heart-stopping yelp. He turned and saw the dog rolling on the ground and biting at his tail.

Wilson pumped another shell into the chamber of the gun and aimed at the dog again. Rags jumped in front of the man and for an instant looked straight into the cold eyes as they drew a bead along the barrel of the shotgun.

"Get outta the way," Wilson snarled.

Carefully, Wilson shifted the gun barrel to one side and Rags realized he must be tracking the dog as it ran for the woods. The boy took one step and launched himself through the air toward the man trying to kill his dog.

Rags seemed to hang in the air for several seconds before his head drove into Wilson's stomach. Just as the two made contact Rags heard the shotgun roar again. His ears rang from the sound of the exploding shell just inches away.

Everything went red as Wilson's fist bounced off the side of the boy's head. Rags slumped to the ground and grabbed the man around the knees.

His arms tightened as the man standing above

him tried to kick Rags loose. Suddenly Wilson's legs went slack and the tall man crumpled to the bare earth.

Rags looked up to see his father standing over him, fists clenched and his face almost as red as his hair.

"E-e-e-yow!" came a scream from just behind him. For the first time Rags noticed Wilson's short friend. He was hopping around on one foot, holding the other in his hand. He had evidently been yelling since the second shot.

"Ah-h-h-h-h, o-o-o-o-o-oh," Shorty moaned loudly from between clenched teeth, "Lewt, you've kilt me."

The boot, which had been ragged before, was now in tatters. Trickles of blood ran from between the fingers holding tightly to the ruined leather.

Rags watched fascinatedly as the little bald man circled them on one foot and cursed fluently.

Rags looked around for Patches, who was now nowhere to be seen. When Rags collided with him, Wilson had been aiming toward a trail that led to the swamp. The boy made his way quickly through the yelling, cursing crowd and into the woods. Carefully examining the well-worn path, he found a drop of fresh blood and then another.

His heart beat wildly as he raced down the trail calling for Patches. If Wilson had hurt his dog bad, he would go back and, well, he didn't know what he would do, but the old snake, he told himself, sure wouldn't like it.

He stopped and called Patches again. In spite

of his concern, a smile was spreading across his face as he remembered his pa standing with fists clenched and eyes blazing over the fallen Wilson. If he could have only seen Pa when he dopepopped the old snake.

Rags' reverie was broken by a whine from a nearby clump of brush. Pushing the leaves aside, he saw Patches sitting there, looking very ashamed of himself. The boy knew he should scold the dog, but his relief at finding Patches was too great. He simply knelt and held Patches close.

Then he remembered to examine the dog for damage from Wilson's shotgun. On Patches' tail he found two spots where the blood had dried.

"Well," he remarked, "looks like both those old snakes left a couple of holes in you."

Patches solemnly licked the boy's nose in agreement.

"Don't try to make up to me, you trouble-maker," he told Patches, laughing. "Thanks to you, we're gonna have to lay low till everything cools down."

A few minutes later the two were slipping quietly through the trees toward the pirogue. For someone hiding out, Rags felt surprisingly good about almost everything.

5

DURING THE NEXT TEN DAYS, Rags and Patches slipped back into their old routine of fishing, exploring and relaxing. There was one important exception: At least two hours every day were spent on obedience commands. Rags did not intend to have another hen house episode like the one that had made them outcasts.

However, his anxiety to see his father, who had become a hero in the boy's eyes with his one-punch knockdown of Lewt Wilson, overcame him. Rags decided to return to civilization and face the consequences of Patches' actions at the cockfight.

The sun had been up no more than an hour when the boy and the dog entered the clearing surrounding the Ragsdale home. It was immediately evident that something was different, but it took Rags a few seconds to realize it was the silence.

As long as he could remember, during the day-light hours there had always been the sounds of chickens around his father's house—the cackling of hens or the crowing of roosters. Now there was only a strange stillness.

Rags saw the cocks were not staked in their usual places as he raced around the house and leaped up on the porch. A bobby pin held a tattered white envelope to the screen door. With a sense of foreboding, he pulled the paper from the rusty screen and tore it open.

He read:

Dear Danny Boy,

I am leaving this note here in case you have not seen Uncle Wash. Go to his house, and he will explain what has happened. This house has too many memories of someone we both loved very much. Be a good boy, and I will be back for you as soon as I can.

Your loving father

Rags read the note again. His father gone? Where? He can't be gone, the boy thought. This is his home.

Patches whined and rubbed against his companion's leg, sensing his distress. Rags absently stroked the soft, yellow fur, still unwilling to comprehend the meaning of the message.

"Well," he said finally, "I guess the only thing to do is go and see Uncle Wash."

Patches barked and dashed toward the fence.

Rags' second shock of the day occurred when they reached Uncle Wash's cabin. Parked outside the picket fence, nearly filled with furniture, sat a flatbed truck. Two teenagers were loading a table onto it.

A dark, middle-aged woman emerged from the cabin with a picture under her arm. Rags recognized her as Uncle Wash's daughter. The old man sat in a chair in the yard, looking at the trees and the cabin, then staring up at the summer sky and the white, puffy clouds that floated overhead.

He noticed the boy almost as soon as he stepped from the trees. Raising himself quickly from the chair with his cane, the old man met Rags at the fence.

"Lawd be praised," he said fervently. "I knowed you's gonna be here today. I tole Leantha we warn't goin' anywhere 'til you got here." His thick fingers touched the boy's shoulder lightly.

"Papa, hurry up now," the woman shouted from the porch, "we almost through here."

The old man ignored her.

"What happened to my pa?" Rags asked. "Where'd he go?"

"Come on here in the yard," the old man replied.

The boy leaped the fence easily, followed seconds later by the dog. "Where are they taking your stuff?" he asked the old man.

Uncle Wash laughed and placed his hand on the boy's shoulder for support. "You sho' do ask lots o' questions widout waitin' for answers. Le's walk around back o' the house."

The man and the boy moved off slowly around the corner of the cabin, the dog following at their heels. As they passed out of sight of the others, Uncle Wash stopped Rags beside a rosebush. Poking at one of the red flowers with the cane in his left hand, the old man spoke softly. "My Pearl planted this—twelve, thirteen years ago . . . right after you's born. Now here it is, full o' purty flowers, and you, you lookin' more like a growed man evah day."

At Uncle Wash's signal they began moving toward the backyard again. "You remember her?" he asked the boy.

"No, sir."

"She's there the day you's born. 'Course yo' daddy had to have the doctor there too. I tole her there warn't no use in her goin', dat the doctor wuz gonna do it all."

The old man was silent for a moment, then chuckled.

"It turned out he'd ast her to come over there. Wanted to make sure dat doctor did it right. Dat Boogah Red nevah did like to gamble. Not then, anyway."

"Where'd he go, Uncle Wash?" Rags asked again.

The old man sat on a small bench underneath a chinaberry tree and looked up at the boy.

"He come over here the day they had dat cock-fight. . . ." A low, rumbling laugh welled up from deep inside the old man.

"I oughta say the day they tried to have dat cockfight and this old Patches dog broke it all up."

Patches' tail thumped happily against the ground.

"He wuz still mad," the old man continued. "He wuz mad at hisself, mad at you, and mad at this dog here. But mainly, he wuz mad at dat Wilson for hittin' you." He paused for a second. "I sure would've love to've seen dat. I mean your pa goin' upside dat piece o' trash's head.

"Well," Uncle Wash went on, "when he come to the part about this dog here, I got mad. I set him down and I tole him how Patches took a snakebite dat 'uz meant for you. I tole him how you and this pup took care o' each other, and it wuz a sight better than he'd been doin' lately.

"He just set there for a spell, then he commenced to cryin'. Then he took on 'bout how sorry he'd been at raisin' you, then he started talkin' 'bout yo' mama. I didn't say nothin'. I jes' let him carry on."

"My pa a-crying?" Rags asked wonderingly.

"There ain't nothin' wrong with a man cryin'," Uncle Wash said sternly. "Your pa held it in him long enough. When a man has a hurtin' in him dat's more'n he can stand, he'll lotsa times hold it in, like it nevah happened. Dat's what your pa did. He nevah let your mama go 'til the day o' dat cockfight.

"After he fin'ly hushed cryin' he jes' set there for a good while, then he stood up and said he wuz leavin'. The next day he come by and give me this money—it's twelve dollars—and said it wuz a down payment for takin' care o' you 'til he come back."

"Where is he, what's he gonna do?" Rags asked.

"He sold them chickens, and he said he wuz goin' to Port Arthur to get a job. Said he jes' couldn't stay around dat house with all them things dat reminded him of yo' mama."

The old man removed a roll of bills from a small coin purse and handed it to the boy.

" 'Cose he didn't know what wuz gonna happen . . ."

He looked at Rags. "Ol' Miz Luker she died last week and Mista Will, he say he gonna sell all this land to some company. They gonna come in here and tear ever'thing down. Even Pearl's flower bushes, I reckon."

"Where are you going, Uncle Wash?"

"Gonna go to town and stay with Leantha. She's been after me for the longest . . . I jes' hated to leave here."

The old black man sighed and scratched aimlessly in the bare earth of the yard with his cane. Patches rested his head on Uncle Wash's knee. The stiffened fingers gently stroked the dog's fur.

"Miz Mack," he said, looking out across the yard to the edge of the forest, "say she take good care o' Veronica."

"What about Bernis?"

"Gonna take him with me, I guess," the old man answered. "You know what dat ol' dog went and done this mornin' when Leantha and those boys started carryin' dat stuff out to the truck? He crawled under dat house, and he ain't come out

44

since. Guess he's like me, jes' old and crotchety and set in his ways."

"Papa," Leantha called from the corner of the cabin, "it's time to go."

Uncle Wash motioned her back around the house with his cane.

"What you gonna do?" he asked Rags.

The boy pondered for a moment. "Guess I'll go look for Pa. Did he say where he was goin'?"

The old man rose stiffly from the bench. "Said some feller told him he'd put him to work on a towboat over at Port Arthur. Didn't say who."

"Well," the boy said hesitantly, "I guess I'll be goin'."

"You jes' wait a minute," Uncle Wash said as he limped toward the back door of the cabin. He emerged a few minutes later holding his fiddle case in his hand.

"Here," he said, thrusting the instrument toward the boy, "you might as well take this. I can't play it no mo'."

"Aw, I couldn't . . ." Rags stammered.

"Take it, boy," the old man commanded, "and you better play it ever' day, too. You hear me?"

"Yes, sir."

Uncle Wash stuck out his hand. Rags, fighting back tears, grasped it in his own.

"You take care o' dat Patches dog and make him mind," the old man said.

"I will," the boy answered.

Both remained silent for several moments. Then Rags, with an effort, looked into Uncle Wash's eyes.

"Well, I guess I better be goin'," he said.

The old man did not answer. He watched silently as the boy spun away, dashed across the yard and lightly leaped the fence with the dog at his heels. Seconds later, the pair disappeared into the trees. Uncle Wash turned and began to call his dog.

6

SEVERAL MILES AWAY, where the highway curved out of the trees of the swamp and into the flat marshland, Rainbow Bridge appeared to be a huge vertical structure on which the tiny, antlike automobiles moved slowly up and down.

As Rags and Patches came nearer the bridge they passed dozens of people fishing and crabbing in the numerous streams that drained the marsh into the Neches River. These happy anglers carefully watched their lines running into the muddy water and yet somehow had time to eat, drink, laugh, and observe the children running back and forth—all the while carrying on a constant conversation in the French-English patois that brought back to Rags a vivid memory of his mother.

From the foot of the bridge, the slab of concrete seemed to disappear into the clouds. Rags, of course, had seen the enormous span before, but it had been from miles away, across the great marsh that stretched from the river to the swamp near the Texas-Louisiana border. Sometimes at night, from the marsh he could see the lights that ran the length of the man-made crossing as they arched against the darkness and over the silent, rolling water below.

As the boy and the dog toiled up the long walkway on the side of the bridge, they were able to look back across the marsh and see the trees that covered the swamp where they had spent so many happy days.

Holding to the handrail to support himself against the backwash from a big truck that swept past a few feet away, Rags looked for some familiar landmark in the faraway tree line. The distance and the haze that hung over the marsh obscured anything he might have recognized. From where he and Patches stood, halfway to the top of the lofty structure, they saw only some dark and distant trees.

When they reached the summit of the bridge, the pair stopped to rest. Rags sat on a thick steel beam and pulled the boots off his feet that had known no heavier covering than a layer of swamp mud for several weeks. His small bundle of clothing lay nearby, along with the case holding Uncle Wash's fiddle.

Far below them, an oceangoing freighter passed slowly, pushed by a small tugboat nestled against the larger ship's side.

"Look, Patches," Rags said excitedly, poking his

head between the railing to peer down. "Pa could be on that little boat right there."

The yellow dog crept cautiously to the edge of the walkway, tentatively thrust his head past the steel bars, whined and began to crawl back from the edge. It was a long way down to the water.

Filled with the elation of travelers near the journey's end, Rags and Patches moved quickly down Rainbow Bridge. The steepness of the descent thrust the boy's body faster and faster until it seemed he was moving more quickly than his legs could carry him. He grabbed the handrail and slowed his progress, arriving in the city at the bottom of the bridge just slightly out of breath.

This side of the river was a surprising contrast to the one Rags and Patches had just left. To the left of the highway, facing the bay, were the docks. Dozens of rickety wooden piers ran out from the docks past the mud flats and shallow water where gulls screamed and dove in a constant search for food. Near the end of the piers, in deeper water, were the boats—all kinds of boats—rowboats, yachts, sailboats, hydroplanes and, more numerous than any other kind, the fishing and shrimping boats.

On the north side of the highway, which by now had become a wide city street, were the businesses that depended on the boats and boaters for their existence.

Boat and motor repair shops, marine supply stores, grocery stores, liquor stores, taverns, restaurants, a movie theater, and a lone building with a sign in front reading, "The Church of the Bay, A

Non-Denominational Refuge," sat waiting for those who returned from the Gulf of Mexico.

The auburn-haired boy gazed in open-mouthed wonder at the bustle and noise of the waterfront. From a nearby open door came the amplified sounds of a guitar. Further down the street, two men stood on the steps of a weatherbeaten building and laughingly shouted at another man attempting to dodge among the traffic and join them.

Rags wandered slowly down the sidewalk, drinking in the sights and smells of the city, all of which were not exactly pleasant. Patches, fascinated by a multitude of odors that seemed to assail him from every side, was busy investigating everything and marking his passage through the city for future travels.

"Hey, get that mutt away from here," shouted a fat man inside one of the buildings just as Patches leaped down from the steps in front. Smoke and loud music billowed out around him as he thrust his head from the doorway and glared at the boy and dog through small piglike eyes almost swallowed by the folds of flesh surrounding them.

They hurried on past another doorway, Rags casting fearful glances over his shoulder at the fat man who remained in the doorway staring at them.

Suddenly, both boy and dog came to a dead standstill. Wafting through the screen door of a cafe came the most delectable smell either could ever remember encountering. The irresistible attraction of the delightful aroma was aided greatly by the fact that neither of them had eaten since before daylight.

Rags looked up into the eyes of one of the largest women he had ever seen. A wide smile shone under her dancing blue eyes. She smoothed down a lock of bright blonde hair and laughed at the pair standing on the sidewalk in front of her.

"Hey now," her voice boomed out at them, "it look like ol' Piggy he wants to have you fellas for lunch."

Rags glanced back at the flabby man. The doorway was empty.

The tantalizing smell grew even stronger. Over the doorway in which the woman stood smiling down at them was a sign announcing "Evangeline's Cafe—Homecooked Food."

Torn between hunger and embarrassment, Rags stood shifting from foot to foot on the sidewalk in front of the restaurant.

The big woman, noting his indecision, asked softly: "Are you hungry, *mon cher?*"

The French phrase, the same endearment his mother had used so often, triggered an automatic response in the boy.

"*Oui, Mam'selle,*" he answered without thinking.

A torrent of Acadian French poured from the blonde woman as she rushed down the steps and took the astonished boy in her arms.

Rags, unable to follow the swift flow of her words, could only nod and smile as she raced on. He knew she was speaking of her family, but he did not understand how this concerned him.

When the woman paused, Rags shook his head. "I'm sorry, you're going too fast for me."

"Are you not Cajun? I thought you spoke French, the way you answer me," she said more slowly.

"My mother was a Boudreaux. She used to talk to me in French."

The woman turned her head and stared across the bay, making a soft clucking sound with her tongue.

After a while she turned back to Rags. "What you mean, you mama used to speak it?"

"She, uh, passed away. In the spring," he responded.

The woman looked at him intently. "Me, I'm stupid sometime," she said. "Come in this house and eat." She started up the steps, then stopped. "And bring that dog, I guess he ain't gonna eat too much anyway."

Inside the cafe were a dozen tables, a few customers and a low bar flanked by revolving stools. Seating the boy at the counter, Evangeline ladled up a bowl of rice and poured several large spoonfuls of spicy shrimp gumbo over it. It was the smell of this fragrant Cajun dish that had stopped Rags outside on the sidewalk.

A plate of meat scraps was provided for Patches. While the two gulped down their first food in several hours, the friendly proprietor questioned Rags and learned of his search for his father.

"I'm sorry, *cher*," Evangeline said when the boy had finished his story, "I don't know your papa, but I'll tell you one thing—if he's working on a towboat around Port Arthur, we sure gonna find out where."

While Rags dug into his second helping of gumbo, the woman circulated among the customers, seeking information on the elder Ragsdale. A few minutes later she slid onto a stool next to the youngster and shook her head.

"Ain't nobody here knows your papa." Noting the crestfallen look on the boy's face, she hastened to console him. "Now don't you worry. Me, I know everybody. All them towboatmen come here to eat. We gonna find him."

Forcing down the last spoonful of the gumbo, Rags hastily refused Evangeline's offer of more food. "I'm about to bust right now," he assured her. "How much do I owe you?" he asked, reaching into his pocket. Most of the money had been carefully shoved into the toe of his boot.

"When you come into this cafe and order something," Evangeline told him laughingly, "then you pay. When I ask you to eat here, then you are my guest, ha?" She took the bill Rags had offered, folded it neatly and placed it in the front of the boy's overalls.

"*Merci beaucoup*," he said warmly.

"You are very welcome," the big woman responded.

Rags slid off the stool and asked for directions to the towboat company.

"Oh, *cher*," Evangeline said hesitantly, "there are so many. Some are big, some have only one little boat." She was silent for a moment. "I tell you what. I'm gonna show you where the two biggest companies are. You go on down there, and if you don't find out anything, come on back here and maybe I find out something by then. That's good, eh?"

Rags agreed it was a good plan. He placed his fiddle case and meager bundle behind the counter, then followed Evangeline out to the street. He was told where two of the largest towing companies were located.

As the boy and the dog started off down the street, the woman called to them, "Don't you forget now, if you don't find your papa, you come on back here. No, you come on back here anyway, even if you do find him. Okay?"

Assuring his newfound friend he would see her later that evening, Rags moved off down the sidewalk. After crossing a side street, he looked back to see Evangeline still watching him, and they both waved. Knowing he had at least one friend in the city made Rags feel better than he had felt since he left Uncle Wash.

In the office of the first towing company, the boy and the dog waited in a corner for several minutes before anyone noticed their presence. When one of the office workers, a prim little middle-aged man, did speak to Rags, it was to tell him to take Patches outside. After doing so, he returned only to find his father was not employed by the company.

"I'm sure glad," he told Patches outside.

The office of the next company was closed when the pair arrived. They wandered around back of the building and eventually found themselves standing on a dock to which one of the towboats was tied. The boat, Rags judged, was at least forty feet long, and he realized the one they had seen earlier passing under Rainbow Bridge had seemed small only in comparison with the big freighter it had been pushing.

They examined the towboat from the dock, Rags resisting the impulse to go on board for a closer look. He had already learned that city people could be awfully unpleasant when they found you someplace they felt you didn't belong.

On the way back to Evangeline's cafe, Rags and Patches investigated several parts of the dock and once even saw a man Rags thought for a moment might be the object of his search. It turned out, however, just to be wishful thinking. The dozens of questions the boy asked along the waterfront failed to turn up even the slightest clue as to the older Ragsdale's whereabouts.

7

THE SUN WAS ALMOST out of sight when Rags
finally decided to halt his investigation for the day.
By the time he arrived at Evangeline's cafe, the
shadows of evening had faded into night.

Rags and Patches entered the kitchen through
a rear door. John, the cook, a wiry, red-faced man
whose arms were almost completely covered with
tattoos, grinned at the boy, exposing a set of loosely
fitting false teeth. He nodded his head in the direction of the dining room.

"She's in there," John told Rags, then went back
to stirring in a large silver pot.

Rags moved on past the cook and entered the
main room, pausing just inside the door to look for
Evangeline. He spotted the bright, blonde hair at a
table in the far corner.

Not knowing what else to do with his dog, he

motioned for Patches to follow him into the press of people who were in various stages of sitting, standing, and dancing to the blaring jukebox. The smell of seafood, spices, and beer hung in the smoky air.

The boy and the dog weaved their way through the dancing couples to Evangeline's table. She was unaware of their presence until Rags reached out a hand and tentatively touched her shoulder. The woman jerked around, the surprise on her face softening into a smile as she realized who was standing there.

A big arm encircled Rags' waist and drew him near the table. "Ah!" she laughed delightedly to the man seated across from her, "I tole you my real boyfriend was gonna come back. What you think about that?"

A row of even, white teeth gleamed under the dark, bushy mustache of the big man. He leaned forward to make himself heard over the music. "So, you gonna be my competition, eh?"

Rags looked at Evangeline. She grinned and winked one eye slowly. Rags, embarrassed, looked at the floor. He shrugged his shoulders, then looked back at Evangeline and her friend, who laughed as one.

"I like this little fella, yeah," the man said, extending his hand to Rags. "My name is Tucker La-Fleur."

The boy took the proffered hand, introduced himself, and accepted Tucker's invitation to sit with them.

Evangeline excused herself and left the table,

returning a few minutes later carrying Rags' clothes bundle and violin case, plus a soft drink which she set in front of him.

"You play the fiddle, eh?" Tucker asked, indicating the instrument on the floor beside Rags' chair.

"Yes, sir," Rags replied, finishing off his cold drink.

"You know some Cajun songs?" Evangeline questioned him.

"Sure," said Rags. Then the big woman rose from her chair, walked to the jukebox, and unplugged it. She waved the protests from the dance floor to silence.

"If y'all wait 'til my fran' here can tune his fiddle, you gonna hear some good music, I guarantee."

Rags, with some misgivings about playing before a crowd, removed the fiddle from its case and plucked at the strings. Surprisingly enough, it was still in tune. Twice he ran the bow across the strings, then broke into "Maiden's Prayer," a lively toe-tapping song familiar to everyone in the room.

The couples on the floor resumed dancing, joined by several others who were attracted by the live music. Rags' nervousness dwindled as the melody spread across the room to everyone's apparent enjoyment.

As soon as he finished the first song, the young musician swung into the opening bars of "Jole Blon," another popular tune among the predominantly Cajun crowd.

Suddenly his concentration was interrupted by a man and woman who stopped dancing and began laughing and pointing beside his chair. There was Patches. The yellow dog could not resist the lively music and was spinning rhythmically around on his hind legs.

One by one, the couples on the dance floor came to a halt to watch the dancing dog. When Rags concluded the song, there was a long, loud applause for both the fiddler and the dancer.

"I'll give you two hundred dollars for that dog," shouted a beefy, red-faced man in a flashy suit and wearing a big, white western hat.

Rags shook his head and smiled. All the money in the world couldn't buy his best friend from him.

The man in the cowboy hat, who obviously had consumed too much beer, wasn't deterred. "I'll make it three hundred," he yelled across the room. The slender, dark-haired woman who hung on his arm giggled and buried her face against his chest.

"I told Louise here I'd buy her a birthday present, and that's just what she needs," he continued loudly, "a dog to dance with her while I'm gone."

The crowd roared at this. Rags, however, was not amused, and in an effort to end further comment he began a waltz which at once filled the dance floor and effectively silenced Patches' would-be purchaser.

Rags' nervousness at performing in front of so many people having by now completely evaporated, he took the opportunity of the slow tune to observe the customers in the room. The fiddle squawked awkwardly as he gave the bow a startled jerk across the strings. Seated at the counter across the smoke-filled room were Lewt Wilson and his running mate, Shorty.

Rags quickly resumed the melody and looked away, trying to concentrate on the music. It was no good, however. His eyes were drawn back to the pair at the bar. The boy could not be sure in the dimness, but it seemed they were both staring at him.

What would they be doing here, he wondered. He tried to convince himself it was only a coincidence, but the memory of Wilson's hateful, snake-like stare at the cockfight kept returning.

As the song ended, Rags once more glanced toward the counter. For an instant his hopes soared when he saw the stools the two had occupied were empty. His relief lasted only until he realized they had moved to a table nearer his own.

"Hey, boy!" the pudgy man's shout cut through Rags' thoughts. The man was right beside him now, weaving from side to side and waving a fistful of bills in his face. "C'mon, fella," he said, spraying a fine mist of saliva into Rags' face, "name your price. I want that dog fer my little honey here." The woman tittered again and clutched his arm tighter.

Rags was suddenly aware of someone standing beside him.

"I tell you what, August," Tucker LaFleur smiled softly as he placed his hand on Rags' shoulder, "If you need somebody to look after Louise while you're gone, I'll take her on the *Bon Temps* with me. I need a deckhand anyway."

August looked at Tucker solemnly, then broke

into a laugh. "Oh, no. I ain't lettin' her go off with one of you Frenchmen." He turned to the woman with a grin. "You might not want to come back at all," he smirked. Louise chortled.

The large man, still ill at ease under Tucker's continuing smile, turned back to Rags and grinned in an effort to show his friendliness.

"Where'd you get this fine animal, sonny boy?" August asked, his face so near Rags that there was no avoiding his heavy tobacco breath and the spectacle of many tiny veins puffing up the tip of his nose.

"I found him," the boy replied, averting his face.

"Found him?" August inquired skeptically. "Found a dog like this? Who trained him to dance, you?"

"Naw, he didn't," came a scornful voice from behind the man, "I did, 'cause he's my dog."

Rags looked up and saw Shorty limping toward them across the dance floor. At his side glided Wilson, his cold yellow eyes fixed unblinkingly on the boy.

"Did I hear you say you wanted to buy this dog, Mister?" Shorty cocked his head and looked up at August.

"He ain't your dog," Rags broke in angrily. Patches, sensing his master's concern, came to his feet with a growl.

"Now Danny Boy," Shorty said with forced good humor, "I told you when I let you keep him I'd have to have him back."

"You never let me have him!" Rags shouted. "That old snake there tried to kill him!"

With a hiss, Wilson stepped toward the boy. The big form of Tucker LaFleur interposed itself between the two.

"Hold on now, boys," he told the three men standing in front of Rags. "We gon' find out just what's happenin' here."

"Now," he said, turning to Rags, "is this your dog?"

"Yes, he is," the boy answered, "and he never . . ."

"Just a minute," Tucker interrupted, "where did you get him?"

"I found him in the swamp. Somebody had pitched him out and he was goin' down in Devil's Sinkhole with another puppy. I couldn't save the other one."

"Ha!" Shorty laughed contemptuously, "I let this boy keep my dog while I was out of town 'cause his daddy's a good friend of ours. Ain't that right, Lewt?"

Wilson, whose cold eyes had never left Rags' face, whispered in agreement. "When Red finds out this little liar took out with our dog, I 'magine he'll blister his backside. He needs it . . . bad."

"What you mean 'our' dog?" Tucker questioned him quickly.

"Why, me and Shorty both own him. Bought him in Louisiana, didn't we?" he said, shifting his gaze to the shorter man.

"Sure did, and I'm gonna take him now,"

Shorty replied, reaching for Patches' collar.

With an enraged yell, he leaped back from the dog, holding his right thumb tightly in his left hand. Patches' teeth had sunk into the offending thumb so quickly none of the others had seen him strike.

"That dog bit me," Shorty moaned.

"I reckon that shows who the dog belongs to, eh?" Tucker observed with a small laugh.

"That little devil turnt him agin me," Shorty cried in a choked voice. He stepped toward Rags and drew back the fist of his uninjured hand.

Suddenly the little man was sliding across the dance floor on the seat of his pants. Big, blonde Evangeline had floored Shorty with one powerful punch. With a growl of outrage, she reached next for Wilson, who eluded her grasp and retreated toward his fallen comrade.

Tucker seized the big woman by the arm and held her against him. "No, no, *chère*," he told her placatingly, "you don't want to mess up your nice floor, eh? Look, that one already tries to drip on it." He indicated Shorty, who was attempting to stanch the flow of blood from his nose.

"I tell you two now," Evangeline muttered threateningly and shook her finger in the direction of Wilson and Shorty, "you gon' get worse than a bloody nose if you do one thing to this boy or this dog."

"'At's my dog," Shorty whined from behind his hand, "and that boy ain't got no right to him. I can sell him or do anything I want with him."

"We can prove that dog's ours," Wilson

growled, helping Shorty to his feet. "A dozen people around the Jericho community will tell you they 'us there when we bought him."

"That's right," Shorty joined in, "and I aim to get the law on this little hoodlum for stealin' my dog. There's laws in this country that pertect a man."

He looked at August again. "You still want to buy this dog, Mister? Three hundred and he's yours. I'll write you out a bill of sale."

"No, you don' understand, my little fran'," Tucker interrupted. "August here is a ver' honest man. He don't buy nothing that is stolen, 'specially when it's stolen from a boy by two grown men who can't even do a good job of that."

August looked into the flashing eyes of LaFleur. A knot of muscles bunched at the corner of the Cajun's jaw and the big, work-roughened hands clenched and unclenched.

"I ain't gittin' in the middle of this mess," August declared as he took Louise by the arm. "C'mon, darlin'."

"Goodnight, boys," Tucker smiled at Wilson and Shorty.

"And I don't want to see either of you in here again," Evangeline added.

"You ain't done with us yet," Shorty yelped. "Shelterin' stolen property is a serious charge. I know my law. You people are gonna find out . . ."

Wilson's furious command cut across the little man's outraged protests. "Let's go," he ordered hoarsely.

Shorty's mouth closed with a snap, and he fell

in behind the slender form of Wilson. Both men pushed through the front door without a backward glance.

"I think maybe we go back to the records now," Evangeline declared, plugging the jukebox cord into the wall.

Rags had resumed his seat and was morosely rubbing Patches' ears. His concern was obvious to Tucker LaFleur and Evangeline.

"Hey, my fran'," the man laughed and clasped his shoulder, "you don' worry so much, those *didans* will not bother you now."

"I don't know," Rags replied, "Ol' Wilson said he would get somebody to swear they had bought Patches. He can do it, too. You can get the trash in Jericho to do anything for a quart of whiskey."

Evangeline and LeFleur joined Rags at the corner table.

"You listen to me," Evangeline said, "people like that don' go to the law. They too busy avoidin' the law. I seen a hundred like that little pipsqueak. Big talk, that's all."

"I tell you though," she continued, "that tall one, what you call him, Snake? Him I don' like a little bit. He got ver' bad eyes. I wish it was him I give this to." The woman waved her fist earnestly in the air to peals of laughter from Rags and Tucker.

Rags felt better knowing he had friends, but one thing still troubled him.

"Why was that red-faced feller so set on buying Patches?" he asked.

"August?" Tucker shrugged his shoulders. "He

is, what you call it, a drummer, a traveling salesman. He has little deal here, little deal there and purty soon ol' August he has the money. He pop off in here about buying the dog for Louise, but you bet if he pays three hundred dollar for something, he knows where he can sell it for a lot more."

As Evangeline agreed the salesman was a shrewd businessman, she rose from the table and walked to the kitchen. Minutes later, she was back with a large dinner tray prepared by John, who over the years had grown largely indifferent to minor disturbances out front.

8

RAGS WAS ONLY HALFWAY through his first big bowl of gumbo when his eyelids began to droop. Evangeline noticed him attempting to stifle a yawn.

"Hey, I believe we got a young fella ready for bed, eh?"

Rags shook his head in disagreement, but it was obvious the long and tiring day was catching up with the thirteen-year-old.

Ignoring his protests, Evangeline gathered up Rags' bundle and the fiddle and led the boy and dog through the still-crowded room and out the kitchen door in the rear of the building. At the top of an outside flight of stairs, she unlocked the door to a small apartment.

Evangeline quickly began making the couch into a bed while she ordered Rags into the bathtub. By the time the boy had scrubbed his body clean and emerged from the bathroom, he found himself and Patches alone in the apartment. With his dog safely beside him, he slipped under the sheet and quickly fell asleep.

Rags didn't know how long he had slept before he was awakened by Patches' whining. The thudding of bass notes from the jukebox still vibrated through the apartment floor, along with an occasional burst of laughter. Patches whined again.

"Need to go outside, huh, boy," Rags said.

Well, the boy thought, rising from the couch and pulling on his ragged overalls, at least he hasn't forgotten his manners. Patches was one of those dogs that seemed to be naturally housebroken, although Rags had been careful to enforce the routine even when they were living in the lean-to in the swamp.

At the bottom of the stairs, they turned right and began moving along the dark, unpaved alleyway. Rags worked his bare toes thankfully into the soft dirt while Patches carefully inspected the exciting smells oozing from dozens of garbage cans and tavern back doors.

Thinking back on the incident later, the boy was never sure whether the encounter was a coincidence or had been planned. Just as he was about to step into one of the rectangles of light that spilled into the blackness of the alley, a shadow loomed in the dirt before him. He jerked his head up in surprise, knowing in that instant who stood on the steps a few feet above him.

It was Wilson. With a strangled cry of rage, the lean figure leaped through the air, his arms outstretched toward the fear-transfixed boy.

Rags felt his face being crushed against the rough, greasy cloth of Wilson's coat. An instinctive fear of suffocation lent him strength as he struck out and attempted to push his way free of the smothering grip of the tall man. Despite the violence of his struggle, the boy was unable to pull loose from the encircling arm.

Suddenly the tightness around his head eased.

"Get the dog off! Get the dog off!" Wilson shouted almost in his ear.

Like a cork out of a bottle, Rags' head popped loose from under Wilson's elbow. Rags tumbled back into the soft dirt of the alley.

From his position on the ground, the boy observed a strange sight. The only light in that part of the dark alley streamed from the doorway just above them. Through this bright oblong ray of light, Wilson whirled around and around on one leg. The other leg ended in forty pounds of dog, securely fastened to his ankle. Shuffling along behind this pair came Shorty, like a wrestler exhibiting his entire stock of holds but lacking the courage to come to grips with his opponent. The little man bent over with both arms outstretched. As Patches made the circle and came back to him, Shorty straightened up, jumped back and aimed a kick at the dog, which missed by at least two feet. The trio passed on into the darkness.

A few seconds later, they entered the light again in the same order, performing the same antics. Wilson yelled over and over, "Get the dog off! Get the dog off!"

By the time the participants in the show made

their second appearance, Rags had regained his feet. "C'mon, Patches, c'mon!" he shouted, pausing only long enough to see the dog relinquish his grip on Wilson. Still whirling, Wilson's momentum reeled him drunkenly into Shorty. Both men sailed across the alley and collapsed into a group of garbage cans.

Running at full tilt down the dark alley, Rags felt, rather than saw, Patches fall in beside him. Behind him, he heard loud voices and the clanging of rolling cans. Looking over his shoulder, the boy saw Wilson silhouetted against the light of the doorway. Then Rags and Patches were around the corner of a building and out into the traffic of the main street.

Luckily for the fleeing pair, the volume of cars and trucks moving along the waterfront street was light. Rags and Patches were across the pavement and onto the docks before the tall, slender form of Wilson appeared under the blinking red and green neon sign of Penn's Tavern, the very place the boy and dog had been chased from earlier in the day.

Crouching over and moving slowly, Rags cautiously inched away from the searching eyes of Wilson. He saw his pursuer disappear for a few seconds behind the corner of the building, then reappear with Shorty beside him.

Rags scuttled along the dock at a faster pace, realizing his and Patches' only hope for safety was to put considerable distance between themselves and the furious men across the street. Just as Rags was beginning to think he had passed beyond the limit of danger, disaster struck.

His only warning was a low growl from Patches

before a brilliant light struck his eyes and temporarily blinded him.

"What're you doin' here, boy?" a high, querulous voice demanded.

Rags glanced over his shoulder. It was as he had feared—Wilson and Shorty had seen him outlined in the flashlight's glare and were now hurrying toward him.

The boy pointed back toward the pair as they scurried through the traffic toward him. "There . . . there . . . they . . ." he stammered. The man holding the flashlight inadvertantly swung the beam toward the approaching men. As he did, Rags, with Patches at his heels, darted around the watchman and bolted for freedom. The man wheezed and lunged for the boy. Rags felt fingernails scratch at his arm before he broke free.

Rags' bare feet slapped hollowly on the dock as he sped into the blackness. Behind him, he heard the babble of loud voices, but he did not stop. He knew that somewhere in the darkness Snake Wilson was coming nearer and nearer.

Suddenly the boy ran out of dock. One instant he had been racing along the wooden platform in full flight, and the next his legs were flailing in the air as he plummeted toward the blackness below.

His first sensation was being unable to breathe. Then as he beat his arms in an effort to surface, he realized he hadn't gone underwater at all. He had done a "belly-buster" right into a mud flat from where the water had receded during low tide.

Rags rose to his knees and attempted to wipe

the sticky mess from his eyes and nose. Above him he heard Patches whining. The dog had stopped before he ran off the end of the dock.

Rags' relief at finding himself and his dog unhurt was quickly tempered by the sound of footfalls approaching on the wooden walkway. Instinctively, the boy grasped one of the pilings and pulled himself under the dock. With a feeling of despair, he remembered Patches above him. The whining dog and the imprint of Rags' body in the mud would be sure giveaways to his whereabouts.

Somehow he had to get the dog out of sight and hope his pursuers failed to notice the depression in the mud flat.

"Patches," he whispered into the darkness above, "come on, boy. Come."

It was a supreme test of obedience. Every instinct of the dog would tell him not to jump blindly. Only complete trust in his master could force him to make the five-foot leap.

"Come," Rags whispered again, the footsteps drawing nearer.

Would he do it, Rags wondered frantically.

His answer came in the form of a soft "plop" as Patches sank into the mud at the end of the pier.

Rags reached out and grasped Patches' collar, pulling him under the shelter of the dock. The footsteps rang out unevenly just over their heads, followed by a moment of silence which was terminated by a loud "Thwack!" Someone else had followed them into the mud.

It didn't take Rags long to determine the someone else was Shorty. The little bald man, whose form the boy could barely discern in the faint glow of distant lights, bounced up from the mud flat.

Swinging his arms wildly and clawing at his face, Shorty broke out in a string of oaths that were muffled by the mouthful of sediment he was vainly attempting to spit back onto the mud flat.

Rags and Patches moved further under the pier as Wilson's sidekick floundered toward the edge of the dock.

The boy froze suddenly as he heard the whispering voice of Wilson right above them. No sound of footsteps had given warning of his presence.

"Ran off the end, eh?" Wilson hissed to his mud-covered partner.

"What the heck does it look like?" came the angry answer. "Here, gimme a hand."

A slow, heavy tread on the boards above announced the arrival of the watchman. Together he and Wilson lifted the little man onto the dock.

From their hiding place under the creosote planks, Rags could see the beam of the watchman's flashlight playing over the churned surface of the mud flat.

"Well," came the squeaky voice of the watchman, "I don't know where your boy went, mister. I sure didn't see him cross the street."

"He ain't my boy," came the choked reply. "He b'longs to a good friend of mine. Run away from home, he did. Mean little devil, his daddy oughtta take a strap to him."

Rags clenched his teeth in anger. Good friend

of my pa's, he thought. When he hears about this, he'll give you another whipping, Snake.

"Well, I'll keep an eye out for him when I make my rounds," the watchman said, his ponderous footsteps moving away.

"If you see him," Wilson called hoarsely, "just tell Piggy over at Penn's Tavern, he'll let us know."

The watchman muttered something unintelligible as the sound of his steps faded into the night.

The silence above was broken as the faint sound of whispering slipped through the cracks between the boards. Rags strained to distinguish the words, but the muted roar of cars passing on the street and the moaning of the ever present wind off the bay were just enough to cover the meaning of the conversation.

He heard Shorty's uneven footsteps move down the dock. A chill ran through the boy. He could not hear Wilson leaving. But then he had not heard him arrive, either.

Rags was in a quandary. Had Wilson left, or had he remained, waiting for his quarry to give themselves away with a sound? To make things worse, the fierce saltwater mosquitoes had discovered the boy and the dog under the dock and were now attacking by the hundreds. Rags, afraid to make any noise, was denied even the pleasure of slapping the hungry insects.

Rags and Patches remained almost motionless under the dock for several minutes. Rags' only movement was to scratch the welts raised by the ferocious mosquitoes and to quietly press Patches back down into the mud each time he attempted to move.

It was during one of these silent struggles with the dog that Rags first noticed his feet were covered with water. The tide was coming in, he realized with a start. Rags assessed his situation. He knew it would be some time before the water level reached its highest point. Even then, there would undoubtedly be plenty of breathing room left under the dock for him. Of course, Patches couldn't be expected to tread water for any great length of time.

His biggest problem, however, was his indecision as to Wilson's whereabouts. Had the man left with Shorty? Although Rags had not heard any accompanying footsteps, he knew the tall man, like a snake, was capable of silently gliding along anywhere.

He can also wait like a snake, the boy thought, remembering the cold, dead eyes whose baleful stare had threatened his and Patches' future.

Rags knew their continued stay under the dock might be in vain, but he was determined to hold out as long as possible. It would take a lot of mosquito bites to be worse than coming face to face with Snake Wilson.

The water was lapping above his knees when the decision was made for him. He had just about determined the wait had been for no purpose when the familiar, hated hiss of Wilson's voice froze him in place.

"How ya doin' down there, Danny Boy?" came the whisper. "'Skeeters kinda bad, ain't they? Ol' Shorty went to get a flashlight. He orter be back purty soon. We coulda used the one the watchman had, but I didn't want him to see what we got in mind fer you. You been a bad boy. You gonna pay fer that."

The voice was so close, Rags imagined he could feel Wilson's breath as it whistled past that yellow fang of a tooth. Rags had managed to restrain himself from fleeing when the shock of hearing Wilson first struck. Now he edged slowly along the length of the pier, hoping to put more distance between them without giving away his position.

As they moved under the dock, the gentle lapping of the swiftly-rising water covered the sound of the boy and dog. Even while he carefully searched for secure and silent footing, Rags realized the mosquitoes had been as bad on Wilson as they had been on him. I outwaited him, he thought with a small grin, and now I'm gonna leave him there to poison all the 'skeeters.

His quick moment of triumph was short-lived, however, as he heard the uneven clumping of footsteps approaching. Shorty must have finally obtained a flashlight, and it would be only a matter of minutes before his and the dog's hiding place was discovered. Even ducking behind the pilings could only delay the searchers for a short time.

Rags was sure that the mud flat sloped steeply as it ran away from the wharf toward the bay. Only fifteen or twenty yards out, the water, which barely topped his knees under the dock, would be over his head. The boy had complete confidence in his swimming ability. Years of living in the swamp had made him almost as much at home in the water as out. The problem was getting into deep enough water before the hunters could close in on them.

Their only chance for escape was to begin swimming immediately, he decided as the beam of the flashlight lanced through the pilings under the dock. Peering around one of the creosote posts, he saw that one of the pair, probably Shorty, was wading toward him, carefully checking behind each piling.

This meant Wilson was still somewhere above, waiting to pounce as soon as he and the dog emerged from under the wooden structure. Rags judged there was less than two feet of water under the dock, hardly enough depth to hide him from the vigilant Wilson.

A piece of driftwood nudging his leg gave him an idea. Taking the short plank, he moved to the edge of the dock and hurled it as far as he could in the direction away from Shorty. The clatter of the board striking a piling was followed a moment later by the swish of rubber soles moving swiftly just above his head.

Taking a deep breath and clasping Patches by the collar, Rags waded quietly out from under the sheltering platform. He gazed through the darkness and discovered Wilson's long form stretched out on top of the dock several yards away. His head hung over the edge as he searched under the structure for some sign of the boy and the dog.

Barely conquering a desire to plunge at full speed through the shallow water, Rags moved slowly and silently away from the dock, Patches swimming easily at his side. The water reached over his waist before he heard a gasp of surprise as Wilson glanced seaward and realized the boy and the dog were escaping.

"Out there, Shorty. I see 'em!" Wilson cried.

Without looking back, Rags dove forward into the water and surfaced with legs and arms pumping. A steady splashing beside him indicated Patches was keeping pace.

For the next few minutes, Rags concentrated on swimming toward a distant light in the bay. As his breathing became more labored, he began to tread water and looked back toward the dock. At first he could see no sign of pursuit. Then he noticed a flashlight bobbing up and down as it moved along one of the piers that ran into deeper water.

He made a half-turn and spotted the shape of a man silhouetted against the lights of the town. This one—Wilson, he decided—was moving down the pier on the other side of the boy and dog.

Rags rose in the water and allowed himself to plunge straight down. His feet touched bottom just as his head went below the surface. Treading water quietly, he moved back toward land until he could stand with his chin above the waves.

He softly called Patches to him. Taking the animal on his shoulders, he bent his knees until the bouyancy of the salt water aided him in supporting the dog's weight.

The tired Patches rested quietly while Rags tried to figure a way out of their predicament. They could return to the dock, but the odds were that they would be noticed, and the boy was unsure he still could outdistance his pursuers.

For the first time, he noticed the boats grouped around the end of each pier. Of different sizes and shapes, there were about a dozen tied to each of the platforms on either side of him.

If he and Patches could make it to one of the groups of boats, their chances of remaining hidden would be much greater. Besides that, he thought, I can't hold up 'ol Fatso here forever.

Sensing the boy's strain, Patches gave him a grateful lick in the ear.

Slipping the animal from his shoulders, Rags began swimming as quietly as possible toward the open bay. Luckily, the wind had risen slightly, causing small waves to whitecap all around them. These would, he hoped, help disguise the splashing as they moved through the water.

Once past the end of the piers, the pair made a wide circle and approached the concentration of boats near Wilson from the opposite side. Although Rags feared the tall man more than his partner, he felt they would be safer in attempting to elude the hunter without a flashlight.

As they swam in among the boats, Rags once again was thankful for the southerly wind that stirred the normally placid water. The waves beating against the hulls of the boats set up a hollow, thumping sound that covered the noise of their arrival.

The boy grasped a trailing anchor line and rested while he decided which of the many boats to go aboard. A small gust of wind stirred the next craft over, and through the dim light coming from the city Rags was able to read the name *Bon Temps*.

He wondered why the name, which meant

"Good Time," appealed to him so. Somewhere, not too long before, he had heard it mentioned. Maybe it was an omen, a sign of good luck, he thought as he swam to the boat and clasped the transom with a shaking hand. He knew his reserve of strength was about finished.

Somehow Rags hoisted himself aboard the little vessel with a minimum of noise. Then, grasping Patches by the scruff of the neck and the back, he hauled the dog aboard. The boy slipped to the wooden deck of the boat and lay there panting, the exhausted Patches lying across his arm. Rags knew the worst enemy he had in the world was very close by, probably no more than a hundred feet away. He made an effort to rise and get under cover, then fell back.

The good Lord would have to protect them now, he thought, just before he collapsed.

9

Rags woke to a gentle rocking motion. He pulled the blanket over his head and dozed again, only to bolt upright a few seconds later at the sound of an engine starting.

By the first orange and pink streaks of dawn, he saw the boat was pulling away from the pier. Wilson was carrying them out to sea! Then he looked forward and to his relief saw not Wilson but the comforting sight of Tucker LaFleur's back over the wheel, with Patches at his side.

It was no mystery now why the name *Bon Temps* had seemed familiar. Rags reflected that LaFleur was getting a new deckhand after all. Drawing the blanket tighter around him to ward off the chilly morning breeze, he lurched sleepily toward the man and the dog.

"*Bonjour, mon ami,*" Tucker smiled in greeting. "You looked tired, so I thought you could sleep."

The big man produced a cup, which he filled with hot, black coffee from an insulated bottle, and handed it to Rags.

The boy sipped the potent brew while Tucker explained how he had found him aboard.

Leaving Evangeline's cafe after closing time, he had crossed the street and reached the pier when he heard voices arguing near the boats. Hurrying forward he found another shrimper, Alphonse Hebert, in a heated discussion with Wilson and Shorty. It seemed the two searchers had boarded Hebert's boat, not realizing the feisty little fisherman was aboard.

The discussion had reached the point of Hebert snatching up an oar and preparing to teach the intruders some manners when Tucker arrived on the scene. Wilson and Shorty, Tucker observed, did not need any encouragement to vacate the premises.

"They ran around me and disappeared like a couple of nutria rats with a big ol' alligator on their tails," he explained. "I didn't realize what they were doing here 'til I found you and this fine pup snoozing away on my deck. It must be that their ears are not so good. Both of you were snoring like rusty saws."

The engine of the little boat chugged steadily as they passed through a cut in the jetties and entered the rougher water of the Gulf of Mexico.

"After I find you here," Tucker continued, "I went back to tell Vangy you okay. Oooh boy, that big woman is on the streets with an iron skillet in her hand. She's plenty mad, gonna knock ol' Snake's tooth out if he's done something to you."

The big shrimper explained how he had convinced the woman not to remove Rags from the boat in the middle of the night.

"She's got one hard head, I tell you that," he said. "Me, I had to promise to watch you ever' second before she agreed to let you make a day out here. You don't mind, eh?"

After Rags assured him he was delighted to be aboard the *Bon Temps,* Tucker continued his explanation of Evangeline's actions.

"Course, she's had some plenty bad thing happen to her. Four, five year ago, her husband and little son were lost at sea during a storm. That boy, he would be about your age. I guess that's why she took to you so fast."

"But, you got to remember," he went on after giving Rags a sharp glance, "women are funny. If you let 'em, they gon' run your life—right down to what you eat and what you wear. A woman sees a man she likes, and she goes after him. Now, what's the very first thing she does after she gets him? Why, she starts to change him from whatever it was she liked about him in the first place."

He's talking to himself as much as he's talking to me, thought Rags.

"I don' believe a woman can help it, though," the big man said, staring toward the empty southern horizon. "Somethin' in 'em makes 'em wanna rule the roost. But when a man lets 'em do it, they don' respect him anymore, I guarantee."

He looked back at the boy, then continued: "I'm tellin' you now, Vangy, she's gonna do ever'-

thing for your own good, whether you like it or not. That's just her way. She can't help it."

Rags considered this. He liked Evangeline a whole lot and deeply appreciated her befriending him. The idea of being tied down in one spot and smothered with affection, though, was really kind of scary. He had experienced a taste of making his own decisions, and he liked it. He sure didn't want to go back to being told what to do all the time.

Rags' daydreaming was interrupted when Tucker dropped the "try" net overboard behind the boat. This small seine, he explained to Rags, was used to determine the number of shrimp in the water. It could be quickly and easily brought aboard and saved a shrimper a lot of time he might otherwise waste while pulling his trawl through barren water.

On the first drop the little net came up with only a single shrimp, but on the second Tucker removed a double handful of the gray crustaceans. Looking over the side of the boat, Rags could see thousands of the little creatures moving through the water. Tucker maneuvered the boat into position and then, with Rags' help, he dropped overboard the big trawl, the boards that catch the current to hold the mouth of the net open and the lines that attach the seine to the boat. The far end of the trawl was marked by a white plastic stoppered milk jug that bounced fitfully over the waves as it moved through the water.

"Now we just wait and hope," Tucker laughed.

Nearly an hour later, they began the arduous

task of bringing the trawl in beside the boat. After this was accomplished, Tucker winched the pocket of the seine into the air with the aid of a small boom swung out over the water.

Rags stared in fascination at the dripping nylon bag. Crushed together inside were shrimp, crabs, big and little fish, and some things the boy had no idea what to call.

As Tucker swung the bag over the deck of the boat and untied the bottom of the pocket, one of the nameless things that looked to Rags like some kind of aluminum snake slithered over the deck toward his bare feet. One swift leap was enough to put him on top of the cabin, safely away from whatever it was.

He watched in amazement as a laughing Tucker snatched the creature from the deck and casually hurled it overboard. "A ribbonfish," he said by way of explanation.

The big man dispatched two small sand sharks by banging their heads against the gunwale of the boat before tossing them overboard. Then, after putting the trawl overboard once more, they got down to the business of culling their catch.

Tucker and Rags donned heavy cloth gloves and heaped a small pile of the shrimp and fish on the culling board—a wooden tray that stretched across the boat over the transom. Here they separated the shrimp into three sizes, jumbo, medium, and bait, and threw the other creatures back into the water, with the exception of the crabs and a few spotted fish Tucker referred to as "specks."

The crabs presented a special problem to Patches. Unlike the rest of the catch brought up in the trawl, these irritable crustaceans were extremely mobile out of the water as well as in. As they worked themselves clear of the wriggling, thrashing pile on the deck of the boat, each of the crabs backed into the nearest corner and assumed a fighting stance with claws outstretched.

Patches, being the self-appointed investigator of all new things, large and small, approached one of the big, blue-pincered creatures warily . . . but not warily enough. With a sudden yelp, he leaped backwards, the crab attached firmly to his nose.

Hardly slowing in his work, Tucker reached out with a foot and kicked the dog's tormentor loose. "Now you know what those pinchers are for, eh?" he chuckled at Patches. The dog, suddenly cautious, chose the middle of the deck, away from all the probable hiding places, to nurse his wounded nose.

The second drag was almost as productive as the first, and it wasn't long after noon when the *Bon Temps* began the return journey home. The insulated iceboxes used for storing the catch were nearly full, and, as Tucker explained, the first boats in received the best prices for their day's work.

The haggling over the shrimp and crabs—Tucker saved the fish for Evangeline's cafe—began before the *Bon Temps* tied up to the pier. A wrinkled old man, his drooping white mustache stained yellow by the years of tobacco that had passed through it, leaned on a pearl-handled cane and watched with careful disinterest as Tucker maneuvered the boat in for docking.

"Well, well," the man said finally, as the *Bon Temps* lay alongside the platform, "I was beginning to worry. I thought maybe you couldn't find your way in."

"Oh no, Jesse James," Tucker answered with a smile, looking around the nearby piers in mock wonderment, "it looks to me like I'm the first one back. You better worry about the mullet you rob here every day."

The big shrimper quickly secured a line around one of the pilings and leaped lightly over the gunwale onto the pier.

"Hey," he motioned to Rags, "come here. I want you to meet John Dillinger."

The boy climbed to the platform and strode to where the two men stood. The man extended his hand and Rags took it, introducing himself.

"And I am Colonel Adrian McDaniel," the man said in his clipped, precise manner. He paused and looked at Rags thoughtfully. "Ragsdale?" he muttered, then shook his head.

He turned to Tucker. "Did you manage to catch any shrimp this time?"

"Hey, boy," Tucker grinned and winked at Rags, "you've seen those cartoons where the bad guy—the villain—is tying the pretty young lady to the railroad tracks just before the train arrives?"

Rags nodded.

"Well, ol' Mac here used to do that in real life. But he had to quit. He was gettin' so old the young ladies were tying him to the tracks," the shrimper guffawed.

"My Gallic friend here," McDaniel replied

dryly, "fancies himself as somewhat of a wit, although it has been my observation he is only about half equipped to play such a role."

Rags looked from one man to the other dubiously. Then, noticing the gleam in Tucker's eye, decided it was just a game the two played.

"I'll repeat my question," the older man stated. "Did you catch any shrimp?"

"Mac, he's what you call a middleman," Tucker explained to the boy, still ignoring the man's question. "He buys the shrimp from the poor fisherman for a few pennies, then he gets rich selling them to stores."

"Any recompense that comes my way is well earned," McDaniel replied archly, "considering I am forced to deal with brigands like you."

"Yes," he continued, turning to the boy, "it's a shame and a pity that a broken old man like myself is required to scuffle in the marketplace all day for a few pennies while a strapping buck like this," —he indicated Tucker—"merely cruises around the Gulf of Mexico, hauling in a trawl occasionally and then wants to deny me a tiny and justified profit.

"Money, which," he proclaimed loudly, shaking his cane in Tucker's face, "if it did not go to me, would be used to enrich the taverns and fleshpots that lie about us here—"

"Yeah," Tucker interrupted, "and if you were twenty years younger, it would be used for that anyway."

The old man broke into a loud cackle, which the shrimper joined. Rags, relieved that the talk had indeed been all in fun, laughed with them, although he was not absolutely sure he got the point of the joke.

"Let's see what you have," McDaniel said finally, stepping aboard the *Bon Temps* with a little effort in spite of the cane.

Tucker opened one of the iceboxes, then turned to Rags.

"You can take the little cooler with the specks on up to Vangy, eh?" He set the plastic icebox on the pier.

Rags lifted the cooler to his shoulder, staggered once, then lurched up the pier toward Evangeline's cafe with Patches at his heels. He wasn't about to let Tucker see how the weight of the box strained him.

Two rest stops and a helping hand from John the cook, who trotted down the alley and took the icebox from the tired boy, saw the fish unloaded in Evangeline's kitchen. John opened a cold drink and placed it in the boy's hand as soon as he had slipped a plate of scraps in front of Patches.

"You bad boy," Evangeline's voice boomed from the doorway of the dining room. Two strong arms enfolded Rags and lifted him from the floor.

"Don't you ever leave again in the middle of the night without telling me," she scolded, "I was so worried about you."

The big woman bustled around the kitchen, heaping a plate with hot food, which she set before the boy.

"Now, I want you to eat every bit of that," she said.

Rags looked at the loaded plate and sighed

inwardly. There was no way he could consume that much food in one sitting, probably not even in two. He picked up the fork and began eating.

As Rags struggled to lower the level of victuals on the dish, Evangeline stood over him touching his hair and rubbing his shoulders. "Oh, I got one big surprise for you," she said happily. "No, you go on and eat, I'll tell you later."

When Rags, with much encouragement, had stuffed down every bite of food he could possibly hold, Evangeline took a chair beside him and delightedly told her news.

"You gon' go live with my sister and her husband," she cried happily. "You can go to school regular, go to church regular, and Richard, that's her husband, he's gon' build a little house in the backyard for Patches. Ain't that nice?"

Rags mumbled noncommitally and forked, with an increasing sense of despair, another pile of mashed potatoes between his lips. At least with his mouth full he didn't have to answer.

Evangeline talked on for a few minutes, outlining her plans for the boy's future before she left for the apartment upstairs. Rags took this opportunity to look for Tucker. He needed advice from someone—in a hurry.

Rags entered the dining room of the cafe, but the big shrimper was nowhere to be seen. Colonel McDaniel, however, was seated at the counter with a bottle of beer in front of him.

"Ah, Mister Ragsdale," he smiled under the yellowed mustache. "Please be seated and join me in a cooling libation—nonalcoholic, of course."

Rags refused the offer but slid onto a stool beside the old man.

"Your friend, LaFleur, will be joining us shortly," the shrimp buyer told him. "He had to wash and anoint his body with scent. It's very unfashionable, you know—" he poked Rags' knee with a bony finger "—to carry on an unperfumed courtship nowadays."

Rags smiled broadly. He loved to hear someone talk so elegantly, and McDaniel seemed to enjoy an appreciative audience.

"Although," McDaniel continued, looking around the nearly empty room, "I really can't understand why anyone would feel constrained to doctor up his own personal aroma just to come to this cauldron of odors. About midnight tonight, the smell of garlic and gumbo and tobacco and alcohol, not to mention good old-fashioned sweat, will be so strong in here that a skunk could walk through the room without attracting notice. Provided, of course, he knew how to do the Cajun two-step."

Before the boy could comment on his observation, the talkative old fellow switched to another subject.

"Ragsdale," he muttered thoughtfully. "You know, that name has bothered me since I was introduced to you this afternoon. I met someone of that persuasion on my last buying trip. Let's see, now . . . Sabine Pass, High Island, Galveston . . ."

"Did he have red hair?" Rags asked excitedly.

"Why, yes . . . yes, he did," the old man answered. "It was in Crystal Beach. But his hair was lighter than yours, more fiery."

"I bet it was my pa . . . Roland?"

"To tell you the truth, I don't remember his being referred to by anything other than Red," McDaniel recalled.

It had to be his father. Rags just knew it. The same name, the same bright red hair; it couldn't be anyone else.

"Where did you see him, Colonel McDaniel?" the boy asked urgently. "Where is Crystal Beach?"

"Crystal Beach? Why, that's a little seasonal community located right on down the highway you see out front. First there's Sabine Pass, then High Island, and then you come to Crystal Beach."

The old man paused and sipped from his bottle of beer.

"Yes," he observed, "one of the few things local politicians ever did right was to see that Highway 87 followed the coastline. Greatly facilitates movement between the coastal cities. Except in bad weather, of course."

Rags was on his feet, nervously trying to leave politely, yet filled with a blazing desire to rush right out the front door and head for Crystal Beach.

"Whereabouts did you see him there?" the boy asked, interrupting McDaniel's geographical monologue.

The old man thought for a moment. "Well, I made several stops that day. Like to keep in touch with all the fishermen, you know. I believe I encountered this fellow at a little store called Becker's, right on the highway. Of course, everything is right on the highway in that part of the country, more or less."

The arrival of two shrimpers who took stools on the other side of McDaniel allowed Rags to slip away from the old man with a quick word of thanks. His mind raced furiously as he entered the kitchen. He knew preparations had to be made for the trip, as much as he wanted to leave immediately. He also had a feeling that Evangeline would do just about everything in her power to stop him if she learned of his plan.

John was slicing a huge ham. His eyes twinkled when he noticed the boy and the dog.

"Had enough to eat, have you?" he chuckled.

Rags swallowed nervously at the thought of more food.

John showed his ill-fitting false teeth in a grin. "Well, if you get hungry later on, or anytime, you just come down here and help yourself. You don't have to wait for me to be here, you're one of the family now."

Rags ducked his head guiltily. He knew the people here—John, Evangeline, Tucker, even Colonel McDaniel—really cared for him and would be upset when they discovered he had left. But he had no choice. He had to find his father. He just had to.

After learning from the cook that Evangeline had left on an errand, Rags climbed the stairs to the apartment with Patches at his heels. The boy stripped off his underwear and mud-encrusted overalls and placed them in Evangeline's washing machine. A few seconds of fumbling with the dials resulted in the machine beginning a wash cycle.

He then filled the tub and stepped into the hot water. After scrubbing thoroughly and shampooing his hair, Rags dried himself and put on his other change of underwear. The boy took the damp clothes from the washer, placed them in the dryer and sat down on the sofa to wait.

"Well," Rags said to the dog, "I guess we ought to lay down and rest for a spell. We got a long way to go tonight." The boy stretched out on the sofa. The effects of the short sleep of the night before and the hard work of the day took hold. Patches sank to the floor beside his master. Soon, he, too, was asleep.

Rags woke in darkness. It had been Evangeline, he guessed, who had covered him with a sheet and slipped a pillow under his head. He sat up and felt Patches' tongue on his knee.

With arms outstretched, the boy moved across the darkened room until his palms collided with the wall. Sliding his hands back and forth, he found and flipped on the light switch.

The clock showed the time to be a quarter past ten o'clock. He knew that Evangeline probably wouldn't return until after midnight. A two-hour start wasn't much, but if he didn't go tonight, he might never have another chance as good as this one.

Rags removed his clothes from the dryer, quickly dressed, and rolled the extra clothes tightly into a bundle. He slung the fiddle case under his arm and was almost out the door before he realized he couldn't go without leaving some kind of message.

A quick search through a small desk in the corner provided paper and pencil. Seating himself on the sofa with a growing sense of urgency, Rags wrote:

Dear Evangeline,

Thank you for the help and something to eat. Please say hello and thank you to Tucker and John. Also thank your sisters husband and his wife, but I am going back home. I will see you sometime again.

Your friend,
Daniel Ragsdale

It isn't really a lie, he thought as he placed the note on the sofa, my home really is wherever Pa is. And if they know I'm going to Crystal Beach, they may come after me.

The boy and the dog slipped quietly down the stairs and stopped to peer in the kitchen door. There was no one in the room. Rags, his sense of self-sufficiency growing every day, realized some food in the bundle would be very welcome during the trip ahead.

He opened the door and followed Patches into the kitchen. "After all," he mumbled to the dog, "John told me to help myself anytime I wanted to."

A check of the refrigerator revealed the ham

slices John had been cutting earlier. Rags gathered a handful which, along with several slices of bread, he wrapped in wax paper and placed in the bundle. A plate of meat scraps went into a paper bag, and a few minutes later the pair were on the highway heading south.

10

RAGS LEAPED DOWN from the cab of the truck, called Patches, and thanked the driver. The engine roared and the old Diamond T rumbled back onto the pavement. The boy watched it slowly move away. He was glad to be back on solid ground. The driver had been nice enough, but, throughout the seventy-mile trip between Port Arthur and Crystal Beach, Rags had been sure the old truck was just about to fly apart in a hundred different directions.

The driver had not been wearing a watch, but Rags felt it was at least two o'clock in the morning. The only lights showing anywhere were those on poles beside the highway. The town itself, providing there was a town, lay in the darkness north of the concrete road.

From several hundred yards away, on the south side of the highway, Rags could hear the slow booming of the surf as it fell upon the beach with peaceful regularity.

The boy and dog found a sandy road leading down to the Gulf. Beach houses, built high off the ground to protect them from hurricane tides, lined the road. As they walked between the clustered beach houses toward the water, the yipping of a small dog in a window somewhere above them pierced the night. Patches stopped to growl an answer, then hurried on.

Once on the beach, they turned and walked along the edge of the surf until they were past all the elevated houses. Rags sat on a large piece of driftwood, removed his boots, and placed them beside the fiddle case and his bundle. He hesitated a moment, then slipped out of his overalls and shirt. Seconds later, the boy and the dog were racing through the frothy white surf.

The cool Gulf water was soothing after the long ride in the creaky old truck. It also took the sting out of the mosquito bites the boy had received while walking down the highway.

Refreshed after several minutes of cavorting in the waves, Rags and Patches made their way back to the log on which the boy's clothing and fiddle lay. But now the mosquitoes formed a painful, whining cloud around Rags' head. As he would slap one, it seemed two more would be stinging somewhere else.

He pulled his clothes on quickly, but this did little to alleviate the savage attack. Not only were his face, neck, and arms unprotected; the savage saltwater mosquitoes were able to pierce through the cloth of his shirt. Rags had to find some way to fend off the predatory insects, and soon. Already the backs of his hands and his face felt puffy from the onslaught.

Rags couldn't very well stay underwater all night, but—of course! He could submerge himself in the sand. He fell to his knees and began scooping a long shallow hole in the soft sand. Patches, always ready for a new game, began scratching beside him.

"No, boy. Dig here," he instructed the dog. Soon they had two eighteen-inch excavations in the sand, one short and the other long and narrow.

Rags placed Patches in the smaller of the trenches and covered his body with the wet sand, leaving the dog exposed above the neck. He unrolled his bundle and removed a shirt which he placed over the dog's head, weighting the edges with sand.

"Stay there," he commanded sternly, as Patches attempted to rise.

Rags did have to laugh at the ridiculous sight, but the mosquitoes weren't resting, and he jumped into the longer hole and began furiously to shovel sand over himself. After a minute of scooping and patting, only his face and right arm remained exposed to the hungry mosquitoes. He pulled the folded shirt over his swollen features and then awkwardly arranged the ragged denim so that it covered his arm. His hand sought the dog's covered head.

Fortunately, the damp sand relieved the itching of his mosquito-stung skin. It would still be awkward, he knew, to remain in one position until daylight, but he would endure a lot before he faced that buzzing cloud of mosquitoes again.

In spite of Rags' firm belief that sleep would be impossible, it was only a few minutes before his breathing matched the slow regularity of the nearby surf. Beside him, Patches whined as he chased, or was chased by, something in his dreams.

11

RAGS SAT UP with a start as the roaring grew louder. He pulled the shirt from his eyes and sat up just as a dune buggy skidded past him and the barking Patches, then slid to a half-turning stop a few feet beyond. Two astonished teenagers in the car gaped at the sandy pair in silence for a while.

Finally, the driver swallowed hard, leaped from the buggy, and trotted to where Rags still sat in the sand. "Are you okay?" he asked.

Rags stood up, brushing away some of the sand as he quieted the growling Patches. "Yeah, I guess so," he answered.

The other teenager joined them and sat down abruptly on the nearby big log. "Boy . . . oh boy . . . oh boy," he mumbled, staring at Rags and shaking his head. The driver, a tall, muscular blond, plopped down beside his companion and grinned at Rags. "Kid, you scared me out of ten years' growth," he said. "If this old log had just a little more sand piled up on it, I wouldn't have seen it. I started to jump the buggy and changed my mind and turned just in time . . . at the same time you and your friend popped up out of the sand."

"I'm glad you did," Rags solemnly observed.

Both older boys laughed, as much in amusement as in relief. Rags didn't much appreciate their humor, but he was glad for company and warmed to his new acquaintances.

The boys, Billy and Ray Pine, were brothers who would soon be returning to college. Billy, the oldest, attended the University of Texas in Austin, while Ray, the slender, dark-haired teenager, would begin classes at Lamar University in Beaumont in a few weeks.

The brothers insisted Rags and Patches accompany them back to their tent further down the beach. The younger boy quickly pulled on his overalls when "hot breakfast" was mentioned. He and Patches and the driver of the old truck had finished the ham sandwiches the night before and now the salt air and the exciting prospect of being near his father were making Rags hungry.

Arriving at the Pines' campsite, Rags was surprised to find five tents erected in a semicircle and several boys moving around a blazing driftwood fire. The smell of coffee and bacon and eggs quickened the boy's appetite.

Just as Rags and Patches and the Pine brothers jumped from the buggy, two cars arrived from the opposite direction. Their passengers, all teenage

102

girls, piled out of the cars, a few walking to the campfire, the rest running into the cold, morning surf.

Delighted laughter floated back from the water. The girls were spending their vacation in a nearby beach house. "The sissies," Ray exclaimed as he scratched some mosquito bites.

The brothers introduced Rags to the rest of the party around the campfire. Learning it would be a few minutes before breakfast, the boy and the dog headed for the water to wash away the night's accumulation of sand.

Rags raced into the surf and dove beneath the waves. Spluttering to the surface, he looked for Patches, only to find the yellow dog surrounded by a group of admiring girls. The boy rinsed the remaining sand off his body and trotted back to the beach. Patches ignored him.

Figuring he already had an old lap dog on his hands, Rags joined the general rush to breakfast.

The boy ate his fill and more, while Patches feasted on a big plate of scraps. As soon as breakfast was over, Rags made his way to the buggy and began removing his bundle and fiddle case.

"Where are you heading, Rags?" Bill Pine asked.

Rags explained he was looking for his father and felt he might learn something of his whereabouts at Becker's Store.

"Why, I'm going right by there," Bill exclaimed. "Hop in, and I'll drop you off."

Rags and Patches climbed in the rear of the

dune buggy, while Bill and Terry, the boy who had cooked breakfast, took seats in the front.

Bill drove several hundred yards down the deserted beach before turning back toward the highway on a rutted road running through saltgrass-covered dunes. Rags noticed only two houses along the road. One had several boards missing from the stairs running up the side and a general look of being long abandoned. The other was a neat yellow cottage perched on eight-foot pilings striped red and white like a barber pole. This cheerful little place was remarkable in that the yard was full of trees like an oasis in the desert.

A few minutes later, the buggy slid to a stop in front of a weathered building marked BECKER'S GEN. M'DISE—BAIT, BEER, GROC. AND TACKLE.

With an invitation for Rags and Patches to join them later, Bill and Terry sped away to meet a group of late-arriving friends. A bell tinkled over his head as Rags pushed open Becker's door.

A sleepy-eyed young man looked up from a newspaper and a cup of coffee as the boy and the dog entered. "Can I help you?" he inquired.

Rags explained who he was looking for and gave the man a description of his father.

The clerk shook his head. "I'm afraid not, buddy. But I just work here part-time. Mister and Missus Becker'll be back from church in a couple hours. Maybe they can help you."

Rags thanked the man and bought a bottle of rubbing alcohol for his mosquito bites and a cold drink, which he took outside. A plan was forming in his mind. If he would be unable to find his father right away, he knew he would need someplace to stay. Another night like the previous one was just about unthinkable, he realized, while massaging alcohol into his mosquito-reddened skin. He would have asked to stay with the Pines, but they had already told him they would not be staying past tonight.

Setting off in the direction from which the dune buggy had just brought them, Rags and Patches reached the sandy, rutted road a quarter of an hour later.

Rags stopped and looked at the dog trotting beside him. "I don't see why you can't help carry some of this stuff now," he said. "You're big enough to do it."

Calling Patches to him, he placed the handle of the fiddle case in the dog's mouth.

"Don't be so lazy," he scolded when Patches looked at him pleadingly. "You just do your share of the work."

Rags started off down the road without looking back. He had gone more than a hundred feet before he glanced over his shoulder. Patches was trotting along behind him nonchalantly with the fiddle case in his mouth. A big grin creased the boy's face.

As they were passing the little yellow house sitting on peppermint candy poles, a voice hailed them. Rags turned to see a pleasant-faced woman of forty or so kneeling in a flower bed.

"Does your dog play the fiddle?" she asked with a smile.

"No, ma'am," the boy replied, "he's just carrying it for me."

His answer greatly pleased the woman, whose
light and airy laugh danced among the flowers and
trees as she rose and brushed the dirt from her shins.

"Are you staying around here?" she inquired of
Rags.

"No, ma'am, that is, well, I don't know . . ." he
answered haltingly, then added, "My father's in
Crystal Beach."

"Oh, I see," the woman said. "Would you like a
drink of water?"

"No, ma'am," Rags replied, "I just had a cold
drink at the store, and, well, I better be goin'." He
turned and together with the dog walked away. The
woman watched them until they passed a bend in
the sandy road.

The deserted cabin Rags had noticed earlier
was only a short way from the beach. The boy looked
in both directions before he left the road. Satisfied
no one could see him, he walked across the sparse
grass of the yard and mounted the stairs. The handrail and several steps were missing, requiring him to
use his hands to climb to the small porch in front of
the door.

It was evident someone had been in the cabin
since the owners had left. The screen door was missing and the jamb was splintered where the wooden
door had been pried open. Shards of broken glass
littered the entrance.

Rags pushed the door open tentatively and
peered inside the almost empty cabin. A strong

musty odor of neglect hung over the big room. A pile of mildewed blankets and bed linen was stuffed into a big wooden barrel sitting under a broken window; the rain pouring in through the shattered pane and souring the bedclothes accounted for the smell.

An examination of the cabinets produced one plastic plate, two case knives, a spoon, and a butcher knife with half the handle missing.

Rags made his way back down the stairs where he had left Patches with the bundle and the fiddle.

"I believe it's just what we need," he told the dog. "It'll take a little fixin' up, but at least we can get out of the 'skeeters."

Patches barked in solid accordance.

Rags rummaged through a stack of lumber underneath the cabin and found several solid pieces. Using lengths of rusty wire, he tied the planks into place over the missing steps. Next, he carried the bundle and the fiddle case into the house and stowed them in the cabinet.

Holding his breath, the boy spread one of the water-stained blankets on the floor and piled the remainder of the bed covers in the center. Drawing the corners of the blanket together, Rags lifted the bundle to his shoulder and staggered down the steps.

After a short walk, he dropped the parcel at the water's edge, removed one of the sheets, and began scouring it with sand. In about an hour, after the sheets and blankets had been cleaned and spread to dry outside the cabin, the boy and the dog arrived back at Becker's Store.

A white-haired woman with rimless spectacles,

Mrs. Becker looked up and smiled as the pair entered the door. When Rags asked for information concerning his father, she cocked her head to one side and answered thoughtfully, "Let's see. I believe there was a feller here like that a few days ago. Ragsdale? I don't know, I never heard his name. He was with some of them fellers off a towboat. Don't know what they were doing down here."

Rags paid for a cold drink and some cookies and continued to question Mrs. Becker about his father's companions. The elderly lady summoned her husband from the back of the store, but he, too, was unable to shed any light on Ragsdale's whereabouts.

The boy knew it might be only wishful thinking, but for some reason he felt strongly his father was nearby. He pondered the situation. If, in fact, his father was somewhere in Crystal Beach, he would surely find him if he asked the right person. They had a place to stay, and if he and Patches had enough food, they could last until someone told them how to locate Roland Ragsdale.

He purchased a bagful of groceries and left the store. He just knew he was going to find his father soon.

12

RAGS WOKE AT DUSK, feeling refreshed. The blankets on the floor made a passable bed and the mosquito stings had at last stopped itching. Before lying down, the boy had stuffed strips of the bed linen into the broken window in the hope of warding off another nighttime mosquito attack. As he examined the patching for signs of an opening, the light from a bonfire far up the beach caught his attention. He remembered Bill's invitation to join the teenagers and suddenly felt a need for their companionship. Calling Patches, he removed his fiddle from the cabinet, carefully negotiated the rickety stairs and set out for the party.

Once on the beach, Rags gave the fiddle case to Patches, and the big yellow dog, who had grown rapidly during the past few months, was the center of attention when he trotted into the firelight carrying the instrument in his mouth. The crowd around the campfire immediately called for a fiddle tune.

"'Sure," said a pretty, brunette girl as she snapped off a transistor radio, "we'd rather hear live music anytime."

Rags found himself propelled into the circle of laughing young people. Patches sat down beside him and offered up the fiddle case. "Okay," the boy responded hesitantly, "you asked for it." He remembered something Uncle Wash always said and repeated it for the grinning faces before him: "If you don't like it, I'm going to finish it anyway."

The teenagers cheered him as he drew the bow across the strings and broke into the melody of "Jole Blon." Several of the boys and girls paired off and began dancing across the sand. There was, however, Rags noted as he changed to a faster tune, one youngster dancing alone. This was a blond fellow less than one year old who, his master realized, would always have to be in the spotlight. "I should have named him Hambone," Rags muttered.

The yellow dog turned and swayed in the firelight, while those teenagers not dancing clapped their hands in encouragement.

Rags continued playing for the appreciative crowd until the call for a picnic supper was given. Everyone grabbed a sharpened stick and began toasting frankfurters, with several of the girls vying to see who would feed the popular dancing dog.

Later that night, after several more tunes and a great many hot dogs, Rags' teenage friends packed up their camping gear ready to leave for their homes. Although Rags hated to see them go, he was warmed by their last gesture. Bill Pine called Rags aside and pressed a few bills and some change into his hand.

When Rags tried to return the money, Bill stuffed the offering into the front of the boy's overalls.

"Look," he explained, "passing the hat is a good old custom, and you and Patches are something special. You could be professionals."

When Rags attempted to hand it back again, Bill chided him in an exasperated tone. "If you give that money back, I'm going to throw it on the sand and leave it there. I mean it."

The boy reluctantly shoved the money back into his pocket.

Bill laughed, and all of the girls made a point of petting Patches and telling him goodbye. A couple of them even hugged the embarrassed Rags. It gave Rags something to discuss with Patches on the way back to the cabin.

For the next several days, the boy and the dog walked the beaches and roads of the little town, seeking news of Rags' father. He became friendly with Mr. and Mrs. Becker down at the grocery store, who seemed to take a great interest in Rags' efforts.

He was also drawn to the Taylors, who, when they were at the beach on weekends, lived in the "peppermint candy house." Their family home was in Beaumont, where Burt Taylor worked. Mr. Taylor, a quiet, friendly man, took Rags and Patches along while he fished in the surf. Mrs. Taylor saw that both of them had plenty to eat and even provided the boy with a castoff swimsuit.

So their stay in the little beach town consisted of more than just a never-ending search for the elder Ragsdale. One incident, which Rags later said he would never forget, occurred one morning as the two were walking down the beach past a large party of adults and children.

Patches, always ready for an adventure, spied a nutria rat emerging from the tall saltgrass of the sand dunes. The rodent, which Rags estimated measured more than two feet in length, snarled once at the barking dog, then together they fled into a tent the women of the party were using for a changing room.

Horrified, Rags listened dumbly as a series of barks, growls, and feminine squeals blended into a symphony of confusion. When the dog and the rat finally passed back through the flap of the tent, they were escorted by several ladies in various stages of undress, each intent on outscreaming the others.

Rags grabbed Patches by the collar as the animal sped past and, seconds later, had him on the other side of the sand dunes headed for the cabin. They were careful to avoid that section of the beach for the next few days.

Another high point of their trips to the beach were the seining parties. Several times they were invited to join fishermen as they pulled three-hundred-foot seines into the surf. Sometimes the "drags," which lasted from thirty minutes to an hour, resulted in only a handful of fish or crabs, while others produced a bounty of speckled trout, flounder, croaker, drum, sheepshead, and other species that kept him and Patches and the Taylors in fresh fish.

The pattern of sun and sand and fishing was altered one morning by Rags overhearing a conversation in Becker's Store.

The boy, as he did almost every day, dropped by to visit with the old couple and learn if they had heard anything of his father.

While talking with Mr. Becker, a bread deliveryman mentioned the Cajun Festival, which would open later that day in Port Arthur. The casual reference triggered a response in Rags. He recalled his mother and father often discussing the annual event, which celebrated the Acadian heritage and culture and often drew more than a quarter of a million visitors to the southeast Texas city.

One of the things that had fascinated Rags as a small child had been the lacquered crawfish shell his parents had purchased at the festival the year they attended.

Rags knew his father, a fun-loving man, would be very likely to attend the festival if he could. Port Arthur might be just the place to find his missing parent.

A hurried conversation with Mr. Becker resulted in the deliveryman agreeing to transport the boy and the dog to Port Arthur as soon as he completed the remainder of his deliveries.

Rags had just enough time to return to the cabin and gather up his fiddle and small bundle of clothes before meeting the deliveryman back at the store.

13

"HAVE A GOOD TIME," the deliveryman grinned as he let the boy and dog off at the parking lot on Pleasure Island, site of the Cajun Festival.

Rags carried the fiddle case under his arm, convinced it would be safer than in Patches' mouth.

Patches scurried toward the flow of the crowd, then slowed to the studied steps of Rags, who gazed at the press of people in open-mouthed wonder. Hundreds of laughing revelers were streaming toward the high, arched gate that was only steps behind a huge banner proclaiming:

CAJUN FESTIVAL—PORT ARTHUR, TEXAS

The aroma of boiling shrimp and crawfish drifted to Rags, who began to tingle with excitement and anticipation as he heard the barkers promote their displays and attractions.

"Don't fail to see the world's largest shrimp,"

came one promising offer from inside the fenced grounds.

"Welcome to de' Port Ar'tur Cajun Fest-i-val," a voice rattled through the public address system.

The boy and dog loped toward the gate. Rags passed two dollars to the man at the ticket booth. Patches bounded past the gate, whereupon a firm but unmenacing hand locked on the dog's scratched collar.

"Whoa, there boy," a uniformed officer just inside the gate laughed at Patches. "You can't go in there undressed."

"You have to have a leash on the animal," the officer explained, turning to Rags.

He reached into a pasteboard box behind him and pulled out a short white cord. "This should hold him," the officer said. "It's the rules that dogs have to be on leashes, but these Cajuns think of everything. They're furnishing ropes for anybody who doesn't have one."

Rags thanked him and arranged to leave his bundle at the gate. "Mighty friendly folks, Patches," Rags observed. "You can't beat nice folks, good music, and plenty to eat."

Caught up in the carnival atmosphere, the boy and the dog sped to the festival grounds. Within an hour Rags had entered the teenage crawfish eating contest, gulping down almost two pounds of peeled crawfish tails, had paid eighty cents for a beef rib for Patches, and had watered the dog at a hose used to wash down tables where Cajun Festival goers savored crawfish delicacies and drank huge pitchers of ice-cold beer.

In the early afternoon, as Rags watched four dizzy youngsters leaving the Ferris wheel, a voice came through the loudspeaker.

"All chil'ren ages twelve to eighteen in'rested in entering the talent contest should go to the main platform where I stan' right now. We're gonna start the contest in fifteen minutes. Sign up, now. No charge. Bring your own instrument, 'les it's a piano. We have that."

The voice continued to boom across the grounds, but Rags and Patches already were headed for the platform.

A small Cajun with a gray mustache and wearing a bright orange beret was calling, "Over here. Register over here to be in the talent contest."

A half-dozen youngsters were already on stage, talking to the master of ceremonies.

Rags glanced at them. A smartly dressed teenage girl cradled a guitar. A taller boy blew lightly into a shiny harmonica. Others shifted from foot to foot holding no instruments.

Rags and Patches bounded up on the steps to the high stage. Rags turned and looked over the expanse of the grounds. People were everywhere, gnawing at corn on the cob, biting into cotton candy, and peeling spicy and aromatic crawfish tails.

The master of ceremonies introduced himself as Alcide Broussard. He described the rules, then told a couple of funny stories. The crowd burst into laughter, but Rags was not paying any attention. He was searching the crowd for his father.

The MC, laughing more uproariously than anyone

in the rapidly growing audience, was handed a list by an assistant.

"Okay, now, first up we have Bessie McNeill and her guitar from Holly Beach, Louisiana. She gon' sing a song accompanied by her sister on the piano. It's all yours, Bessie."

The MC walked to the side of the platform. "Better tie that dog, son," he said to Rags. As the girl started her song, Rags tied Patches loosely to a stage post.

Bessie completed her rendition of "Blue Eyes Crying in the Rain" to thunderous applause. "Picks like Willie Nelson and sounds like Billie Jo Spears, don't she folks?" Alcide Broussard said as he returned to the microphone.

"Next up is Patsy Melancon and her accordion. You're in for a real treat," he announced.

Patsy worked her arms like a baby bird attempting first flight, then pressed heavily on the keys, forcing out music that soon had the audience swaying.

Three other contestants performed before Rags heard his name announced. He had become so enthralled with the gaiety he had momentarily forgotten he was in the contest.

"Danny Ragsdale," the loudspeaker blared again.

Rags yanked his fiddle from the case and stepped hesitatingly to the microphone.

He eyed the crowd, glanced at Patches lying a few feet away and caressed the strings with the bow. Patches watched intently.

Within seconds Rags was into a ringing rendition of "Jambalaya." The tempo electrified the crowd. One straw-hatted man of about fifty began to stomp his right foot. He wrapped his arm around the generous waist of a woman nearby and guided her to the open area between the stage and the crowd. Their experienced feet, arms, and torsos seemed to blend together as they swirled about, dancing to the music of Rags' fiddle.

Soon there were a dozen couples merrily kicking up dust as they whirled about.

Rags deftly moved from "Jambalaya" to "Alons —dans 'cest Colinde" without missing a note. The dancing crowd grew. Those on the stage were tapping their feet and clapping their hands.

Suddenly laughter and more clapping burst from the viewers to the left of the platform. One man, pointing unnecessarily, asked, "Would you look at that?"

On his hind feet, straining against the rope, was Patches, trying to dance despite the restraint of the leash.

"Turn that dog loose," someone yelled, and the crowd picked up the chant, "Let him dance. Let him dance."

Rags continued to play, laughing aloud at Patches.

Alcide Broussard patted Patches, quickly untied the rope, and released him. Patches was instantly on his hind feet, promenading across the stage toward Rags. His front feet pawed the air, and his mouth wagged open in what appeared to be a big grin.

Around the stage Patches danced while Rags

continued to play and the din from the crowd increased.

Rags raced smoothly into "Under the Double Eagle." Another contestant began playing his harmonica in harmony with Rags. Bessie McNeill picked up the tempo with her black guitar and Bessie's sister joined in on the piano.

By the time Rags had reached the solo part of the song, he and Patches had completely won over the laughing, dancing, yelling, clapping crowd.

When Rags drew forth the last note from the fiddle, pandemonium let loose. Patches dropped to his all-fours and joined Rags at the microphone. The boy bowed to the applause, which continued until the delighted master of ceremonies finally called it to a halt.

Four other youngsters performed in the next few minutes. Each was greeted by an appreciative audience, which included Patches, who had to be restrained from dancing during the remaining musical numbers. Rags thought surely one boy, who performed magic tricks, would win the contest, even though Bessie McNeill had been awfully good.

As the boy talked quietly with some of the contestants, he glanced at the judges' table and saw the master of ceremonies looking at him, while another judge pointed to Patches and laughed.

Alcide Broussard walked to the microphone.

"Folks," he began, "you will have to agree this was the most talented bunch of performers we've ever had at our Cajun Festival." The crowd responded with a thunderous applause.

Holding up his hands for quiet, the master of

ceremonies continued, "But we can only name a third, second, and first place prize.

"Here to announce the winners is the president of the Cajun Festival Board of Directors, Boss Cajun Terrell Neveaux. Boss Cajun Neveaux," he gestured toward the short, stubby man to his left.

"Ladies and gentlemen and little Cajuns everywhere," Neveaux announced. "You have seen the best teenage talent in all of Cajun Land. Since the governors of Louisiana and Texas have declared Pleasure Island the capital of both states during this festival, I guess that makes these teenagers the very best in the two states." He paused and looked across the hundreds of upturned faces in front of the platform.

"Now, for the winners. And they're all winners, you know. The judges had a mighty hard time, but we've picked three winners."

Neveaux studied his list.

"Third prize of ten dollars cash and this gold cup goes to thirteen-year-old Tommy Hebert. C'mon out here little Cajun Hebert."

Tommy Hebert was the young magician. He shook hands with Mr. Neveaux, accepted his money and prize, and smiled a huge smile. The crowd applauded warmly.

Neveaux leaned toward the microphone. "Congratulations Tommy." Neveaux paused and looked over the crowd. "Now for second place and a prize of this cup," which he lifted to show the audience, "and fifteen dollars cash money." He looked at his written notes. "Second place winner is that 'Blue Eyes Crying in the Rain' girl, Bessie McNeill."

Bessie skipped forward happily and accepted the cup and money, then bowed to the yelling crowd.

"Ladies and gentlemen, the winner of first prize," said Boss Cajun Neveaux, "is this overalled boy with the fiddle . . ."

As the audience was already clapping and yelling, few could hear Neveaux as he screamed, ". . . that boy with the dancing dog, Danny Ragsdale."

Rags went forward to Neveaux, followed by Patches. The man handed him the greenest twenty-dollar bill he had ever seen. As the crowd cheered, Rags looked at the money, then at the winner's cup. The golden cup read, "Cajun Festival Teenage Talent Contest, First Place."

Rags touched the inscription and looked at Neveaux. Then he turned to Patches, who pawed at his leg.

Rags knelt beside his faithful friend and wrapped his arms—one hand still holding the cup—around the tail-wagging dog. The applause had ceased for a moment, but now it resumed in earnest. Patches dashed to the edge of the stage and acknowledged the cheering with a chorus of loud barks.

He then trotted to the judges' table, stood on his hind feet and barked loudly several times. Rags walked over to join Patches, stammering, "Thank you."

Boss Cajun Neveaux walked to the edge of the stage and conferred with a man wearing an "Official" badge on his chest.

Neveaux stepped back to the microphone. "Ladies and gentlemen," he said. "We have one more prize to give."

He turned to Patches, patted him firmly, and led the dog to center stage. Neveaux held up a blue ribbon that said "First Prize." He leaned over and tied the ribbon around Patches' neck while the crowd applauded once more. The dog dropped to his feet, pranced to the edge of the stage and barked loudly again. The crowd loved it.

14

THE ATTENTION SHOWN Rags and Patches at the Cajun Festival grew quickly embarrassing to the boy. His back was sore where huge hands had slapped him, accompanied by dozens of voices calling, "Great going, boy," or "Wonderful talent. Yes, sir, wonderful talent."

One man offered Rags one hundred dollars for Patches but succeeded only in reminding Rags of August at Evangeline's cafe. Another wanted to give Rags fifty dollars for the fiddle and bow. He wondered where people got that much money.

Rags was appreciative of his sudden fame, but as the afternoon wore on he yearned more and more to be back at the beach alone with Patches. His initial reason for being at the festival—to look for his father—had been lost in the excitement of the day. There was no sign of his father among the crowd.

Surely, had he been present, he would have come forward at Rags' performance.

When Rags heard a voice say on the public address system that it was four o'clock and time for another contest, he turned glumly to Patches and said, "We had better be going, boy. It's a couple of hours back to the beach."

They were in the parking lot outside the festival grounds when Rags saw it. There was no mistaking that coat. The black, moth-eaten garment fell loosely from the bony shoulders of Lewt Wilson, who was kneeling behind a car. His running mate Shorty crouched at his side. They were no more than fifty feet away. Worse, they had seen him.

Rags began to run. Patches raced with him. Rags looked over his shoulder, hearing Wilson yell, "He saw us. Git 'em."

The weight of the fiddle case, his bundle, and the first prize gold cup in his hands impeded Rags' speed. The two men were gaining. Rags darted around a car onto a street. He looked left and right for safety or assistance. His hesitation was his undoing.

Around one side of the car came Lewt Wilson. Rags turned away. Closing in on him in the other direction was Shorty. Rags braced himself, extending the fiddle case in front of him as a shield. Shorty collided headfirst with the case, staggering off to one side. Immediately, Patches was upon him, snarling viciously.

Rags felt the rough fingers of Wilson close around his neck. He dropped the gold cup and bundle. Shifting his feet, he sent an elbow crashing into

Wilson's midsection. Rags heard the air rush from Wilson's lungs and felt his hands go limp.

Shorty was screaming. Patches, his teeth sunk into an ankle, had thrown the man down in the gravel. Rags dropped his fiddle case and bolted in the direction of the struggling pair, grabbing for one of Shorty's arms.

As he did, he heard Wilson behind him. Rags turned to see Wilson with the fiddle in his arms. The tall man began to run through the cars.

"You snake. You no-good snake," Rags cried.

Shorty's screaming pierced the air. "C'mon, Patches, c'mon," Rags yelled.

The dog released his hold on Shorty and scampered behind Rags, who was now following Wilson through the parking lot. The black-coated figure darted around a car, then back out on the street. As he turned to look over his shoulder, he ran right into the hands of a waiting policeman.

The officer grabbed Wilson by the collar of his ragged coat. "Hold it, buddy, just hold on here," the uniformed man said to the struggling Wilson. A few yards away, Shorty was on his knees, beating the ground with two doubled fists.

The bald man wept. "That's all. Never again." Shorty looked up at Wilson through wet eyes.

"I've had it, Lewt," Shorty pleaded. "I've gone along with you on this boy and that dog and that's it. Because of you and that dog, I've been shot in the foot, almost kilt, I've been attacked twice by that animal, I've been punched out by a woman, knocked into a bunch of garbage cans, I've run off a dock and purt near kilt myself again, I've been beat with a fiddle, and now," he sobbed, "I'm goin' to prison. I can't take this no more."

Shorty rose to his feet, held out his hands in a gesture of surrender and staggered to the policeman, who was still holding Wilson. "Lock me up, officer. Git me away from this man and that dog." Shorty sobbed heavily.

"Why you sneaking polecat," Wilson snarled. The policeman shoved Wilson against the car and snapped a pair of handcuffs on his wrists.

"Let me go," Wilson demanded. "I haven't done anything. That man there," Wilson nodded his head toward Shorty, "tried to steal this boy's fiddle. I was just gettin' it back for him."

"You're a lyin' rat. A snake!" Shorty blubbered through his weeping. "I done no such thing."

"Okay, hold on, you two. You've both got some answering to do," the policeman said.

Another policeman had by now joined the group. He led Wilson and Shorty to a nearby squad car, Patches following.

Shorty groaned as he fell into the police car. "Lock me up. Put me away. I don't want to be near that dog."

Rags, having retrieved his belongings, thanked the policemen again, then whistled to Patches to join him. The dog still stood by the police car, growling softly at Shorty.

"We'll take care of these two," one of the policemen promised Rags, "but we'll need to know how to get in touch with you if we need to. What's your address?"

"You can reach me at Becker's Store in Crystal Beach," Rags responded.

"Good. Be careful now," the officer urged.

Outside the Cajun Festival parking lot, a young couple in a convertible stopped to offer Rags and Patches a ride. Fortunately, the couple in the convertible were going all the way to Crystal Beach on this bright, hot late afternoon.

Two hours later Rags and Patches were deposited at Becker's Store. The boy left Patches standing outside in a steadily-increasing breeze, while he went inside. Rags purchased food for himself and for Patches, throwing in as a bonus for the dog a meaty bone. He used more than six dollars of his prize money.

Just after Rags and Patches left the store, Mrs. Becker turned on the television behind the counter to the following news:

> Tonight in the Gulf of Mexico, there are early reports of a tropical storm. The United States Hurricane Center has predicted the storm will reach hurricane proportions of seventy-five miles per hour by tomorrow. There is, of course, no way to determine which course the hurricane will take. Should it reach hurricane force, it will be the third hurricane of the season. Its name is Claudette.

After a pause, the newscaster said,

> Now in the local news, the opening day of the Cajun Festival has been declared a great

success by sponsors. Police reported only one incident. There was an altercation outside the festival grounds involving the winner of a talent contest. Two men were taken to police headquarters. One was released after posting bail.

Across the screen moved Lewt Wilson, covering his face as he walked out of jail.

As a light rain fell that evening on his adopted beach home, Rags, cheerfully unaware of Wilson's release, playfully cuffed a drowsy Patches under the jaw. A friendly growl had barely escaped before Patches fell fast asleep.

The boy looked admiringly at the trophy he had won and at Patches' blue ribbon tied to it. Then he lay back on his blankets. Thinking how proud his father would be, Rags too was soon lost in dreams.

The next day, Rags noticed the surf growing rougher. Because he saw numerous fishermen at the beach and on the piers, he felt no alarm. What the boy did not know was that fishermen always caught enormous redfish during the days preceding a storm in the Gulf.

Rags and Patches stayed mostly to themselves. The boy pondered his future, wondering if he should go elsewhere in search of his father. "But we enjoy the beach so much, and this is the last place Pa was seen," Rags said to Patches as they romped along the surf.

Having decided to stay, Rags examined his food supply four days later and found it very low.

"Well, we better go to Becker's," he told his companion.

At the store, Mrs. Becker welcomed them. "How you been doing, Rags? Haven't seen you in several days. But I read about you and your dog winning those prizes at the festival. You could have told me when you were in here that day, you know."

Rags apologized for the oversight.

"It's all right," the woman continued, "Anyway, I have some good news. There was a man in here looking for you not more than a half hour ago who said he had news of your father."

Rags almost jumped with impatience. "Really, Missus Becker? What did he say? Has he seen my father? Where is the man?"

"Well," she replied, "he seemed very eager to find you. I described the way to your place. I drew him a little map. I'm surprised you didn't see him on your way here. Did you walk up the beach or take the road?" Rags told her he had walked the beach, so he probably would have missed whoever it was looking for him.

"What did he look like?" Rags asked.

"Oh, he was sorta tall and skinny. Didn't have many teeth," Mrs. Becker said. "And, oh yes. He had on this old black coat, which I thought was odd . . ."

"What is it, Rags?" Mrs. Becker asked in alarm. "You look like you've seen a ghost." It was true that Rags was pale. He stumbled back into a rack of food. "Rags, what's the matter?" Mrs. Becker demanded.

"I . . . I . . . I . . . I think . . ." Rags attempted. Rags hurried to the front door of the store. His immediate concern was for Patches. The dog ambled to its feet as he opened the door. Finding Patches safe, Rags walked back into the store. He bought essential items, filling one sack, then paid a puzzled Mrs. Becker.

"Rags, you worry me. Is there anything I can do?" she wanted to know as she gave the boy his change.

"I guess not. Thanks anyway," he replied.

"But the man who was here. Is there anything wrong?" she pressed.

"If it's who I think it is, he's no friend of mine," Rags answered.

Leaving the woman with an undecided and quizzical look on her face, the boy joined Patches outside the store. "Patches," he began, "we're in trouble again."

Rags heard the door open behind him. He looked around, seeing Mrs. Becker. "Rags! There's a hurricane—Claudette—brewing out in the Gulf. It's not supposed to come in here, but do take care."

Rags thanked her and started to leave. Mrs. Becker called to him again. "Also, Rags . . . you have to watch for snakes when hurricanes are coming. Snakes go to high places when tides rise. So be real careful."

Rags thanked her again.

Rags and Patches crossed the highway and walked toward a lane that led to the beach. Had he looked over his shoulder, he might have seen the straw-hatted head of Lewt Wilson peering from behind a stack of boxes at the side of the store. Wilson rubbed his hands together, a cruel smile creasing his face.

Rags and Patches returned to the beach shack

without incident. Once inside, the boy barricaded the door. Bewilderedly, Patches watched his master's actions. The dog had never seen the boy act so peculiarly.

"Patches," Rags said, after pushing the wooden barrel, in which he had found the bedclothes, against the door, "we have to lay low for a while. I believe Lewt Wilson is after us again." The name brought a growl from Patches.

"I just don't see how he got out of jail," Rags told the dog.

Two days passed. Rags spent most of his time looking out the patched window of the cabin. He kept the broken-handled butcher knife with him at all times, determined to defend himself and his dog should Wilson appear.

Near the end of the week, Rags noticed the surf was higher than he had ever seen it. He was becoming less concerned about Lewt Wilson. "Maybe it was someone else that looked like him," Rags told Patches. "I guess it's been pretty foolish us hiding out in here. C'mon boy," he said, "let's go play in those big waves."

Patches ran into the surf and Rags laughed loudly. Behind a sand dune at the rear of the beach shack, a head appeared, then disappeared.

"See, I told you they were here. I'll split the money with you when we sell that dog," croaked the voice of Lewt Wilson. "Lucky fer us I heard the boy tell the cop where he wuz stayin'," he exulted. Wilson spoke to a heavyset man wearing a red and yellow cap.

"Cain," Wilson snorted, "this is our lucky day. That boy and dog are holed up in that shack. I've been watchin' 'em ever' day, waitin' fer you to git out of jail. What we'll do is wait fer them to git back in the cabin. Then we'll sneak up thar and git 'em."

"Lewt," Cain said. "You are really obses . . . obses . . . you really want to catch that dog, don't-cha?"

Wilson rubbed his hands together and breathed a low whistle through his teeth.

An hour passed. Rags and Patches still romped in the water, although the waves were much higher than an hour before. Rags saw black, menacing clouds approaching from the south. Light rain began to fall.

"Git down. Git down," Wilson hoarsely whispered to Cain as the boy and dog ran toward the house.

"I'm gittin' wet, Lewt," Cain whined, wiping water from his face.

"Shut up, you fool. They'll hear us," Wilson said, clouting the man across the head.

"You don't have to do that, Lewt," Cain pleaded. "You didn't have to hit me. Why'd you hit me?"

Wilson didn't answer. He crawled carefully up the dune to see if Rags and Patches had arrived at the shack. Just as his head topped the dune, the boy and the dog ran up the stairs.

"Okay, let's go. But quiet, now," Lewt warned.

The two men slithered over the wet dune. They halted at the bottom of the sand hill, then Lewt sprinted across the opening between the dune and the house. He arrived under the cabin gasping for breath.

He looked around for Cain. His face twisted in shock as he saw his partner moving across the open ground on hands and knees, slapping a cupped hand into the sand.

Wilson stomped his feet in exasperation and disgust. He motioned violently at the engrossed man who crawled nonchalantly beside the dune.

Finally, Cain leaped to his feet, a beaming smile on his face. He held something in his hands as he ran toward Lewt.

"Look what I got," he whispered loudly. "It's a fiddler crab. I caught him crawlin' in the . . ."

Lewt Wilson yanked the cap from Cain's head and slapped the stunned man across the face.

"Lewt?" Cain bawled. "Look what you did, Lewt."

Cain had dropped the crab. The little beach scavenger backed away from the men, its claws up in the air.

"Ah, Lewt. Look what you've gone and done. You made him mad," Cain moaned.

Wilson stepped forward and crushed the crab with his foot.

Cain gasped in disbelief.

"Now you shut your mouth. We got to git that dog," Wilson seethed. "That's what we come fer. Now let's git with it."

"Hey, it's dry under here," Cain observed. "I think I'll just rest a spell and git dried off," he sighed as he sat down.

"Git up from there, you clod," Wilson warned.

"If you don't listen to me—" He eased a knife from the pocket of his black coat and flicked open the blade.

Cain stared at the knife. "Well," he stammered, grinning weakly at Wilson, "now that you esplained it to me."

"That's better," Wilson growled, "now, follow me."

Wilson crept toward the stairs. Cain followed closely behind, looking one way, then the other. He jerked up his head and humped his shoulders, as if trying to remove a crick from his neck. "Stop that jumpin'," Wilson scolded.

Cain curled up a bottom lip, sulking.

Wilson, his face masked in viciousness, tiptoed closer to the stairs, remaining in the growing darkness under the building. He heard no movement overhead. "Now don't say another word. I don't want to hear one more peep out of you," Wilson warned again. Cain flinched.

As Wilson prepared to step from under the house, Cain saw something sliding along a wooden beam above his partner's head.

"La . . . Le . . . Lew . . . Lewt . . ." Cain clamped his lips, brought his hands to his mouth, then froze in his tracks.

Wilson reacted to Cain's muttering. He whirled angrily, in the same instant catching a glimpse of the snake darting its head below the beam. The reptile speared itself at Wilson. To the terrified Cain, the snake appeared to slide in slow motion toward its victim.

134

Fangs plunged deeply into Wilson's vulnerable neck.

He choked, trying to scream. No other sound escaped as he sank to his knees, grasping the snake with two trembling hands. Wilson looked at Cain through glazed eyes.

Horrified, Cain stood motionless, his hands still cupped to his mouth.

Wilson's eyes closed and his hands slipped from the reptile's body. As he pitched forward, the snake dropped to the ground and glided under the pile of old lumber from which Rags had constructed the steps for the cabin.

Wilson moaned once, then shook violently.

Cain at last removed his hands from his mouth. There was only one thing he knew how to do in the face of disaster. That was to run. He bolted from under the house, racing toward the sand dune. As he scrambled over the hill, Wilson raised himself to his knees and called hoarsely, "Cain! Cain!"

The portly man disappeared.

Wilson grasped a board and hoisted himself unsteadily. He staggered from under the cabin, lurching from one piling to another. The stricken man clinched his teeth against the pain and righted himself. He fell again, then crawled.

"I'll git you Cain," he sobbed as he reached the sand dune.

At the top of the mound, Lewt willed himself to his feet.

Weaving like a tall weed in the wind, he squinted his eyes and attempted to peer through the rapidly gathering gloom. Far away, he saw three tiny Cains scrambling over a sandy hill. He swore once more, his face twisted in agony.

Suddenly he toppled over and slid to the bottom of the dune. His body shook violently and a hand clawed the sand. He gave another shudder, and was still.

Rags and Patches had heard nothing. When he returned from the swim in the pounding surf, Rags had stripped off his bathing suit, slipped on his overalls, and dozed off, unaware of the strengthening storm. He had not even heard Patches whimpering in his sleep.

15

RAGS SLEPT MUCH LONGER than he intended. He raised himself from the cot and rubbed the dog.

"Patches," Rags said, "I guess that swim relaxed us a little too much. It's getting real dark outside."

Rags walked out on the porch of the cabin, followed by Patches. He shivered as he saw the frothing surf rolling over what had been a beach only hours before. Patches barked twice. Like a warning, Rags thought.

"We better head up the beach and see what's going on," he said to the dog.

Buffeted by the strong wind and a stinging rainstorm, Rags and Patches slogged up the muddy road to the Taylors' cabin. Mr. Taylor was nailing a piece of plywood over a front window. His wife loaded bags into a pickup whose bed was partially covered by a plastic shelter.

"What's going on, Mister Taylor?" Rags asked.

"My gosh, boy. Are you still here?" Mr. Taylor responded, looking with concern at the wind-whipped trees in his yard.

"We had no idea you were still down here. We just came in a while ago to close up the house and get what we can in the pickup truck. We hadn't seen you lately."

The tone of Mr. Taylor's voice alarmed Rags. He glanced at Patches, then back at Mr. Taylor, who by now was calling to his wife.

"Jean, better hurry up."

The deeply tanned woman raced down the steps, clutching a portable radio. "Listen," she called to her husband, holding the radio close to her ear. They joined Mrs. Taylor under the shelter of the raised cabin. From the radio Rags heard:

Hurricane Claudette is now said to be less than four hours from landfall, twenty miles northeast of Galveston, Texas. Winds from the season's third hurricane are reported to be more than eighty miles per hour.

"You mean it's coming in around here?" Rags yelled at Mr. Taylor.

"Come on, boy, we've got to get moving. You'll go with Jean and me in the pickup. The dog can ride in the back," Mr. Taylor hurriedly decided.

"But I've got to get my things," Rags pleaded. Water had already risen to within a few yards of the Taylor's house. Rags shivered, dressed only in overalls, then started for his shack.

Rain began to fall in torrents. "No time, Rags," Mr. Taylor beckoned. "We've got to get going." The man's voice knifed through the fury of the wind, which seemed to become more intense with each passing second.

Mr. Taylor gently but firmly led Rags to the cab of the pickup. Rags crawled in beside Mrs. Taylor.

Mr. Taylor raced to the rear of the truck and placed Patches in the bed.

Rags looked through the rear window at Patches, who was trying to find a dry spot among the bundles in the back of the pickup.

"Here," Mrs. Taylor said to Rags as she wrapped a large beach towel around the boy's shoulders. "This will dry you some."

"But my fiddle. Uncle Wash gave it to me. I've got to get my fiddle," Rags begged.

"It's not worth the risk," Mr. Taylor warned.

To Patches, the fiddle was worth taking a risk. As the pickup lurched toward the main highway, the dog leaped to his feet with a start.

The dog looked through the pickup window and barked twice. Rags could not hear over the noise of the radio and the sounds of the storm. Patches barked once more, then bounded from the back of the pickup.

As the dog raced for the beach shack where he and Rags had spent so many hours, he could imagine the fiddle case hanging from the wall. Patches would get it for Rags.

The yellow pickup turned northeast and inland

off the beach road as Patches pushed open the door of the shack. The three people in the cab heard the radio announcer say:

The Hurricane Center has officially declared Hurricane Claudette will reach the Texas coast by 9 P.M. tonight. Winds at time of landfall will be approximately ninety miles per hour. Center of the storm at landfall is officially designated at a location twenty miles northeast of Galveston, Texas, at longitude 94.3 and latitude 30.4. The eye of the hurricane is expected to pass over Bolivar Peninsula and the community of Crystal Beach. Evacuation of that area has been ordered by the Texas Department of Public Safety. Red Cross workers and officers of the Department of Public Safety are assisting in the evacuation of the area.

"It's good they were there to help the Beckers," interjected Mrs. Taylor.

The hurricane's center at 6 P.M.—that was twenty minutes ago—was located forty miles southeast of Galveston at longitude 94.3 and latitude 29.9, moving toward the Texas coast at twelve to fifteen miles per hour. The hurricane, until noon today, had remained stationary about one hundred miles southeast of Galveston. The National Hurricane Center said the storm, which increased in force while remaining stationary, began its coastward movement shortly after noon with winds increasing from eighty miles per hour at 2 P.M. to eighty-five miles per hour at 5 P.M.

All persons located along the coast twenty-five miles southwest of Galveston, and twenty-five miles northeast of Sabine Pass, are to evacuate the coast and seek safety and shelter inland.

Mrs. Taylor, almost in tears, said, "Please hurry, Burt."

"Be quiet, Jean," he snapped. Then, abashed, he said, "I need to get the report on the road conditions, honey."

Highway 87 between High Island, Texas, and Sabine Pass, Texas, is already closed to traffic. Those evacuating the Bolivar Peninsula area are urged to utilize Highway 124 northward to Interstate Highway 10. The Galveston Ferry has already been closed. Both lanes of Highway 124 from High Island to Winnie on Interstate 10 will be utilized by northbound traffic. Officers of the Texas Department of Public Safety have already closed southbound traffic on Highway 124 between Winnie and High Island.

Burt Taylor neared the intersection of Highway 87 and Highway 124 leading to Winnie. As the newscaster had said, Highway 87 to Sabine Pass was barricaded. He turned north on Highway 124 toward Winnie.

Just beyond the beach community of High

Island, Rags turned to look into the back of the pickup. "Patches! Where's Patches?" he cried. Rags twisted completely around in the pickup seat and peered into the back of the pickup.

"He's gone, Mister Taylor! He's gone! Patches isn't back there!" Rags yelled.

"He's probably up under the bundles," Mrs. Taylor said calmly.

"No, he isn't. He's not there. You've got to stop, Mister Taylor," Rags pleaded.

"We can't stop now, son. I'm sure he's back there." Mr. Taylor attempted to comfort the boy.

Rags was determined. He grabbed the steering wheel of the truck. "Please stop."

Mr. Taylor pulled to the side of the road. "We'll check, son. I'm sure Patches is there."

Mr. Taylor slid off the seat onto the wet ground. Rags followed immediately behind him, then streaked past. The boy vaulted over the tailgate of the truck and into the back, where Patches should have been.

Mr. Taylor, wiping the rainwater from his face, peered into the pickup bed shelter. "Well, son?" he asked. Rags turned to the man. The boy's face was drained of all color.

Mr. Taylor realized Patches had jumped from the back of the truck. He didn't have time to wonder why.

"He'll be okay, Rags. He'll find safety. Animals are better at that than humans. You'll see," he consoled the boy.

Rags climbed from the back of the pickup. His

shoulders sagged. He looked longingly toward the beach. He allowed Mr. Taylor's strong hands to lead him back to the pickup cab. Rags' drooping head and his trembling chin revealed his thoughts.

"Oh, Patches. Patches," he half muttered. Mrs. Taylor looked knowingly, sorrowfully, at her husband. She reached across and lightly caressed his shoulder. Then she nodded northward where safety awaited. Mr. Taylor pulled back on the road. The woman increased the volume of the radio while Rags wept within.

16

PATCHES HAD KNOWN danger before. He had almost disappeared under the ground in that place where the trees grew all around and the other dog had not been with him afterward. It was the first time he had ever seen the boy.

Then the thing from the water hurt his leg. The boy had carried him in his arms to where the big dog lived. There was more pain, but always the boy was there to touch his head and reassure him.

Even after the loud noise had hurt his tail, the boy had found him hiding and had taken him to the boat and had pushed them across the water to the place where they ate and where his tail stopped hurting.

Now, as one of the blankets the boy had stuffed in the window trembled and snapped before the force of the howling wind, Patches waited for his master to return.

The dog had wanted only to retrieve the fiddle —it was his job to carry it. He had leaped from the pickup, raced back to the cabin and made his way to the big room, where he found the fiddle case lying on the upturned wooden barrel.

Seconds later, he picked his way down the swaying steps with the case handle firmly between his teeth and set out for where Rags and the other people should have been. There was no one there when he arrived.

Confused, Patches had returned to the shack. As he pushed down what had been a sandy road hours before, the wind-roughened water splashed over his back. With his head held high and the case clenched securely in his jaws, the dog reached the cabin and what he hoped would be safety.

The journey from the bottom of the stairs to the little sun deck at the top was as difficult as anything Patches had ever done. Three of the old planks Rags had wired as steps had been torn loose and now hung by one end under the staircase, twisting and slapping against each other. Twice the brutal wind and the rain-slickened boards had joined to send Patches sliding through a gap in the steps and down into the swirling water below. Each time, the determined young dog managed to keep the fiddle case above the rapidly rising torrent.

At last Patches had climbed to the porch and made his way into the big room, where he had sunk to the floor and lay panting.

Day gave way and the dog peered down at the rising Gulf water, which was now less than a foot from being inside the cabin. The wind had torn away parts of the roof, and almost solid sheets of water now poured into the old beach house.

Patches felt the structure shaking. He barked but was answered only by the howling wind. A loud, splintering noise accompanied a shifting of the cabin's floor. The big, wooden barrel, which Rags had used as a table, fell to its side. Another section of the roof collapsed inward.

Patches grasped the handle of the fiddle case in his teeth and crawled inside the barrel, just as the remainder of the roof gave way, sending a cascade of boards and shingles to the floor of the building.

Suddenly the cabin rolled to one side and Patches felt the barrel being tossed into the air. A rush of cold water slammed against the stricken dog's eyes.

Patches huddled in the bottom of the big barrel and waited.

17

Burt and Jean Taylor stared into the growing darkness, the headlights of their pickup glaring off the big car in front. Rags sat quietly, looking out the window as they crept past rain-filled roadside ditches. The middle-aged couple knew no words would console the boy.

Because of the heavy traffic, it had taken them more than an hour to make the normally twenty-minute ride from the beach to the small town of Winnie on Interstate Highway 10.

Burt Taylor eased the loaded truck into the flow of cars, trucks, and trailers bound northeast toward Beaumont, as Mrs. Taylor searched the radio dial for the latest weather bulletin on Hurricane Claudette.

The traffic sped up on the main highway, and half an hour later the weary occupants of the pickup were approaching the outskirts of Beaumont.

Taylor slowed, then came to a stop behind a long line of red taillights.

"Looks like a roadblock up ahead," he observed.

For the first time since he discovered Patches was missing, Rags spoke. "What does that mean, Mister Taylor?"

"They're probably giving instructions on the best route inland. They won't let us go home tonight," Mrs. Taylor predicted before her husband could answer.

A policeman waved a flashlight just ahead. As he drew alongside the officer, Taylor rolled down the window. The policeman looked into the vehicle. "We're ordering everyone to go north as far as they can drive tonight," he said, shouting over the noise of the beating rain. "There's no telling what the storm will do once it comes inland. It could turn this way. So please keep on driving."

The instructions did not surprise Burt Taylor. He rolled up his window and turned to his wife. "Well, we expected that. We'll just keep driving and try to make Lufkin."

Rags had never heard of Lufkin. "Where is it?" he asked. "Lufkin, I mean?"

"About 100 miles north of here," Mr. Taylor answered. "I don't think the hurricane will come in that far. It will run out of steam once it's touched land."

Mrs. Taylor patted Rags' leg. "We don't have to go that far. We have some friends with a farm about fifty miles north of here. We'll stop there for the night."

"Hey, that's a good idea," her husband remarked. "Al and Sheila will be happy to have us. I'll bet a lot of their friends from down here have the same idea, though."

It was after midnight when the truck pulled into a driveway leading into a wooded area. "Is this the farm?" Rags asked.

"It is," Mr. Taylor answered. "We'll be welcome here."

Several cars were parked in front of a farmhouse nestled among the trees. Rags and the Taylors dashed to the house, shielding their faces from the rain with the large towel Mrs. Taylor had brought from the "peppermint candy" house, now so far away.

Mr. Taylor banged on the door. It was immediately opened by a man with rumpled hair. He grabbed Mr. Taylor by the arm. "Get in here, Burt."

"Thanks, Al," Mr. Taylor said.

Al looked over the newcomers. "Anybody else with you?" he asked.

"Nope, this is the crew," Mr. Taylor said, as they entered the house.

Inside, Rags surveyed a large room with giant windows, which were being lashed with rain. There were several adults, two teenage boys, and two teenage girls in the room. A television was on in the corner and a radio could be heard in another section of the house. Rags walked toward the sound of the radio and found two men and a woman sitting at a kitchen table, listening to the latest weather bulletin.

Within a matter of minutes, Mr. and Mrs. Taylor had introduced Rags to everyone in the house and had explained how they had brought him from the beach.

As Mr. Taylor explained to their host, Al Mayes, the conditions of the night driving from Beaumont, Rags stood at the large picture window and, with the illumination of the lightning flickering across the sky, watched the rain slash through the trees and fall to the earth.

The boy felt something cold and wet touch his hand. He looked down to see a large, orange and white dog standing at his side.

Mr. Taylor watched the boy rub the dog's back. The man who had rescued Rags from the beach turned to Mayes. "The boy had a dog at the beach. We had it in the pickup, but it must have jumped out. We didn't have time to get it," he explained.

Mrs. Mayes walked over to Rags. She held a pair of trousers and a shirt. "Why don't you go in there and change," she said. "I'll hang your overalls to dry."

Thanking the woman, he changed in the bathroom and returned to the large room to find the dog who earlier licked his hand.

"I think he's more at home with animals than with people," he heard Mr. Taylor say. Everyone was gathered in front of the television.

"They'll be broadcasting all night," Mr. Mayes said.

Rags listened as the newscaster reported the latest developments:

Landfall for Hurricane Claudette came just after midnight. The center of the hurricane went inland northeast of Galveston on Bolivar Peninsula. The National Hurricane Center reported Claudette's winds were in excess of ninety miles per hour at landfall. Hurricane Claudette has caused tides of five to seven feet from south of Galveston to a point forty-five miles northeast of Galveston near Sabine Pass. Authorities believe all residents in the target area of Hurricane Claudette have evacuated.

"Not Patches," the people in the room heard Rags mumble.

The boy thought of Patches as he walked back to the window to look into the night. Hold on, Patches, he thought, I'll get to you. I'm coming. You'll see. I'll get away from here tomorrow. You're alive and I'm coming to get you. No storm is going to keep us apart.

One hundred and twenty-five miles to the south, at Crystal Beach, the dog heard nothing.

18

RAGS WAS ASSIGNED a small couch near the front windows of the farmhouse for sleeping. He awoke the next morning to gray daylight and the sound of thunder rattling the big windows.

As he looked about the room at the other sleeping figures, Rags heard the radio.

He rose from the couch, still dressed in the trousers and shirt Mrs. Mayes had given him the night before, and walked to the kitchen. The Taylors and the Mayeses sat around the kitchen table drinking coffee. The two women were in housecoats, the men disheveled in their clothes of the night before. Their faces, although lined from the long night, hinted at signs of relief.

"Morning, Rags," Mr. Taylor smiled.

"Good news, Rags," said Mr. Mayes. "The hurricane turned across open country and then into Trinity Bay. There's quite a bit of damage along fifty or so miles of the beach . . ."

Mayes stopped, shaking his head. How stupid, he thought, not to remember the boy's dog had been left on the beach at the very location the storm came ashore.

One of the Mayes boys entered the kitchen. "What's the news, Dad?" he asked.

Mayes recovered himself. "David, it stayed away from the big cities. Galveston, Port Arthur, and some of the other places along the beach have a lot of water from rain, but the seawalls kept the tides out. The hurricane moved across Trinity Bay and did a lot of damage at Anahuac, then it headed up the Trinity River valley and did some damage at Liberty. Other than that, though, it looks like Miss Claudette is losing her steam as she goes farther inland. It's going to cause a lot of rain all over the state, though," Mayes said. "I'm sorry, boy. I didn't think," he added, to Rags.

"It's all right, sir," said Rags. "I'm just worried, is all."

They handed Rags a cup of coffee.

Throughout the morning, Rags watched the steadily falling rain. A small lake at the rear of the farmhouse was filling rapidly, but the farmhouse, built on a hill, was in no danger.

The men, the older boys, and Mrs. Mayes left the house for a couple of hours during the morning to tend the farm animals.

Upon their return to the house, Mrs. Taylor

mentioned that they might be able to return to their home in Beaumont.

"We can't go back for a couple of days," Mr. Taylor said to his wife. "The news says the rains have caused a lot of flooding in Beaumont and Port Arthur. Let's just hope our homes are safe. The main thing is, though, that we're okay. Anyway, there's probably a lot of water over the road down that way. It's best we stay here for a couple of days."

Mr. Mayes, shaking water from his hat and wiping dry his face, said, "Y'all are welcome to stay as long as you like. You, too, Rags," he said to the boy.

Rags walked to the corner of the house where the large, orange dog lay. Rags knelt beside the dog and whispered softly, "I'm not staying here, dog. They're good folks, but they don't understand. I'm heading back to find Patches. He wouldn't let any old hurricane get him. He made it. I know he did."

The dog rubbed its nose against Rags' leg.

Early that afternoon the rain outside the farmhouse lessened. Rags thought over what Mr. and Mrs. Taylor had said about staying at the farm for another two days.

He walked around the house. All the others were sitting on a screen porch at the back of the farmhouse, watching the rain fall. Rags hurried to the bathroom and changed from his borrowed clothes to his own dry overalls.

When he left the bathroom, Mrs. Mayes was standing in the adjoining bedroom. She held out a pair of green sneakers and a pair of socks. "Want to try these on?" she asked. "They're old. They belong to David. But I think they'll fit." She handed them to Rags, who thanked her. "Why don't you keep that shirt on, too," she pointed to the garment Rags had removed.

Mrs. Mayes started toward the back porch to join the others. "We'll be eating shortly," she said. "Come out back and join us on the porch, if you like. I think the rain is letting up."

As soon as she left the room, Rags quickly put on the socks and shoes. He walked to the door leading to the screened-in back porch and looked at Mr. and Mrs. Taylor, Mr. and Mrs. Mayes, and the others. He wanted to thank them. But he knew they wouldn't allow him to leave if they knew his intentions.

Rags nodded at their turned backs and walked quietly to the front door. Easing it open, he slipped outside, leaned against the door as it softly closed, and took one long, deep breath. Then he raced past the cars parked in front of the house, stopped once to look up the lane, and sprinted toward the paved road.

Rags knew the direction in which they had come the night before. Some of it, anyway. He remembered the pickup had turned left off the highway into the lane leading to the farmhouse. That meant his first turn was right. Rags hadn't understood clearly the course taken by the hurricane, nor the dangers it might pose to him on his way to look for Patches, but he knew there was no hurricane at Crystal Beach now, and he was headed back down there at last.

He walked for what seemed to be several miles.

The rain pelted his body, and he whispered a thank you to Mrs. Mayes for giving him the shirt and sneakers to wear.

Three times during the afternoon Rags waved at passing vehicles. None stopped. My feet can do it, he thought.

He ran. He trotted. He walked. Then he ran some more, his chin tucked into his chest to shield his face from the rain.

Toward evening, he topped an incline and saw ahead an intersection where the small road on which he had been traveling joined a larger one. A little store with a gasoline pump in front sat beside the intersection. A single exposed light bulb burned in front.

Rags stepped inside. A small woman rocked in a caneback chair in front of the counter, a book in her hand, a walking cane across her lap, and a cat sleeping at her feet. Her hair was coiled into a tight bun at the back of her head.

She examined Rags closely, then reached over and took up an empty can. She looked at the can, looked up at the boy, then spat into the can.

Rags stood before her, dripping water onto the wooden floor.

"Quite a night for you to be out, isn't it, sprout?" she asked, her pursed lips barely moving. She placed the can on the floor.

Rags cleared his throat. "Can I buy some crackers and cheese and an orange drink?" he asked.

"If you've got the money, you can buy what you want," the old lady said. She laughed shortly and, with the help of the cane, pried herself up from the rocker and shuffled over to the big, glass-fronted refrigerator.

Taking out a hunk of cheese, the old woman carved three big slices. "The drinks are over there," she nodded toward a cooler. Rags selected a bottle of orange soda water.

When he turned back to the old woman, she was wrapping the cheese in paper and placing it in a sack. She reached behind the counter and took the lid from a small cracker barrel, counted out ten crackers and dropped them into the bag.

"Fifty-five cents," she said. "You have fifty-five cents?"

"Yes, ma'am," Rags answered. He counted out the change and thanked her.

"Better open that bottle before you leave," she said, and handed Rags an opener. "You can eat that here if you want to," she suggested, and smiled for the first time.

Rags smiled back. "Thanks, but I've got to be going," he said.

"Crackers will get wet," the woman observed.

"That's true," Rags acknowledged. He sat down on the floor in front of the cooler and started on the crackers and cheese.

"Must be somethin' mighty important, to be headin' out in this weather and at this time of night," the woman said, looking at the large clock over the counter. It was six o'clock.

"Yes, ma'am," Rags agreed, taking a sip of his orange drink.

Presently, he asked, "Do I go to the left there to get back toward Beaumont?"

"That's right," she nodded. " 'Bout fifty miles."

"Thanks," said Rags, adding his empty bottle to those in the rack.

Rags opened the door and glanced back into the store. The woman was shaking her head.

"Hardheaded," she muttered, and pushing her glasses farther up on her nose, she resumed her reading.

Outside, the rain was falling steadily. Rags ducked his head and marched into the night.

Hours later, Rags, shivering from the wet cold, surrendered to his fatigue. The wet sneakers had rubbed his feet raw and the boy realized his strength would not carry him much further. Observing a bridge just ahead, he slid down the embankment toward the river which went rushing under.

Exhausted, Rags curled up on the sloping bank under the shelter of the bridge, folded an arm under his head, and soon was asleep.

The boy didn't know how long he had slept when he was awakened by the sound of the river crashing against its muddy banks. He rose to a sitting position, peered through the rain and realized how near he was to the dangerous onrush of water.

Up the wet bank Rags scurried. He paused to regain his sense of direction and began to trot down the edge of the highway. "I will get to Patches," he vowed.

Minutes after he emerged from beneath the bridge, Rags waved at a passing van. The vehicle

158

slowed to a stop, Rags chasing to catch up with it.

The passenger door of the van opened. Rags looked in at a young man, alone in the front.

"Where you headed?" the driver asked.

"Beaumont," replied Rags. "Get on in out of that rain, boy," the young man said.

The vehicle pulled back to the highway. The driver, who introduced himself as Mark Young, was wearing only cutoff jeans, a shirt chopped off above the midriff, and a pair of sandals.

Young was from Dallas and was going into Beaumont to find wallpaper hanging jobs in the area. "There's always a lot of work after homes are flooded," he explained.

"Beaumont and Port Arthur aren't flooded too bad, are they?" Rags asked.

"No," said Young, "but there's enough at the beach area, around Anahuac and in some of the smaller places to keep me busy. My paperhanging equipment is there in the back." He pointed to the wallpapered rear of the van.

About an hour later, Rags stepped from the vehicle and waved thanks to Young for the ride to Beaumont.

"Only one more hour to the beach," Rags thought.

He looked at the noonday sky and decided it might be clearing, since the clouds were no longer as dark as they had been earlier. It was difficult to believe a hurricane had struck less than two days before.

Rags hadn't walked far along the highway before he was offered another ride, this time in the back of a truck hauling sandbags. The driver, a man in a khaki shirt and trousers and hip boots, told Rags he was taking the bags to a stretch along the Trinity River.

At Winnie, Rags thanked the driver and started again on foot.

As he walked through the community of Winnie, Rags felt excitement building. He moved faster, urged by the anticipation of finding Patches. For the first time in two days, the sun peeked from behind a cloud, then as quickly hid again.

Rags was almost trotting now.

A few yards ahead, he saw a man climbing into the cab of a huge truck. On the flatbed of the vehicle was a road grader.

Rags raced toward the truck and shouted to the man in the cab.

"Are you going to the beach?" he yelled.

The man turned over the big truck's engine. "Well, I'm going to deliver this machine to the beach area," he responded. "They're beginning to clear the highway down there."

"Can I ride with you?" Rags pleaded. "I've just got to get to the beach."

"They won't let you go down there," the man replied. "They have a roadblock up. They're not letting anyone in. There's snakes washed everywhere, houses scattered around, maybe even people. Naw, son, they won't let you in down there."

"But I've got to go there. My dog Patches is there. Please, give me a ride. They'll let me in."

The urgency of the boy's voice touched the

truck driver. He shrugged his shoulders and motioned for Rags to get in.

Rags hopped in the truck, a broad grin on his face. He brushed his hand through his rust-colored hair, which was already drying.

"I'll never forget this, mister," Rags said. "You help me get to the beach so I can find my dog, and I'll make it up to you, I promise."

Rags was surprised at himself talking so much. His happiness at being near Patches was so great he couldn't stop.

"He's a great dog, mister. He's smart, too. He can dance and he can really make you laugh. I found him in the swamp. Pulled him out of the quicksand. He saved me from a snake one time . . ."

The man, amused, looked at Rags, but said nothing.

The boy continued to chatter excitedly.

As they neared the beach, Rags saw the water was only a few feet off the highway. "How high did the water get at the beach?" he asked the driver.

"At least a couple of feet over the highway," said the man, "but it's going down now. They're starting to clear the roads this afternoon. That's the reason I have this grader on the rig. The operator is down at the roadblock, waiting on me.

"They're not going to let you in, you know," he added.

"They'll let me in," Rags blurted. "They wouldn't keep me away from Patches."

The boy rolled down the window on his side of the cab. The sun had broken clear in the sky, and the air was heavy and hot. Scattered rain clouds were moving rapidly northward, following the path of the hurricane which now was reduced to a storm far inland.

The truck slowed, and Rags saw a uniformed patrolman and a man wearing a hard hat standing beside a yellow pickup and a car with a long antenna. The pickup and car were pulled up to a wooden barricade.

"That highway patrolman isn't going to let you in there, now, boy, dog or no dog," the driver predicted.

As the truck stopped, Rags opened the door and climbed from the cab. They were still a few miles from the Gulf. As a matter of fact, Rags realized, the truck had stopped at almost the exact spot where he had discovered Patches was missing from the Taylor pickup.

The truck driver strolled over to the patrolman and the other man, followed by Rags.

"Got your grader, Lem," the driver said to the man with the hard hat.

"I see you have, Harm," said Lem. "About time."

Lem Milstead, the grader driver, turned to the patrolman. "Officer Duncan, this here is Harm Adams." The two men shook hands.

"What 'cha got there with you, Mister Adams?" Officer Duncan asked, nodding to Rags.

"Says his name is Rags," replied Adams. "He's looking for his dog. Left him at the beach Friday before the storm struck. Says he's going back to the beach for the dog."

Officer Duncan nodded his head, putting one hand into a back pocket. "Where's your family, son?" he asked.

"I don't know where my pa is. My ma is dead," Rags said, looking first into the face of the patrolman, then down at his tattered sneakers.

"Say, I know this boy," exclaimed Milstead. "Saw him at the Cajun Festival. He can play the thunder out of a fiddle, I'm telling you. Got a dog that can really dance, too," he added.

Lem walked over to Rags and placed a hand on his shoulder. "Was that dancing dog at the beach?" he asked Rags.

"Yes, sir. I'm going back to get him. He's waiting on me. He needs me." Rags looked over their shoulders, down toward the beach.

Duncan, Adams, and Milstead looked at each other. Rags tried to keep the doubt in their faces at a distance.

"No. Patches is okay. Let me go see," he cried, fear now replacing the certainty he had maintained for so many hours.

"Son," said Officer Duncan. "I'm not supposed to let anybody past this roadblock. The highway is covered with sand and boards and glass and parts of houses and no telling what else. No one has been down there yet. Helicopters and airplanes have been going over since about noon yesterday, surveying the damage, and it's a big mess. There's nothing alive down there except snakes. The water has just this morning begun to run off the highway. No, I can't let you in. I'm sorry. If anything happened to you, it would be my fault."

The other men were silent. They looked at the ground, Adams toeing the dirt at his feet.

Rags bit his lip, his fists doubled at his sides. He fixed his gaze on the eyes of the patrolman.

"Sir, I was always taught to be polite and respect the word of the law. I've walked and hitched rides for a hundred miles since yesterday. I walked in the rain and slept under a bridge just to get back here to find my dog. You have to let me through. I've got to find Patches."

Tears shone in his eyes, but Rags blinked them back.

"Are you going to let me in?" he asked the patrolman.

"Son, I—" the officer stammered.

Lem placed a hand on the sleeve of the uniform. "Officer, isn't that your radio going in the car?"

The patrolman looked at him quizzically. "I don't hear a radio," he said.

Adams looked at Duncan, then at Lem, then back at the patrolman. "Sure it is, officer," he said.

Lem walked to one side of the patrolman and Adams moved to the other. Each man took one of Officer Duncan's arms. The three started walking to the patrol car.

"Officer Duncan," Milstead said as they neared the car marked "Texas Department of Public Safety," "we have to think this over. That's some spunk the boy's shown."

The patrolman looked from one man to the other. "Look, I feel for him as much as you do," he said. "I'd love to let him through. But I have my orders."

Rags watched the men, wishing he could hear their conference.

After a while, he saw the patrolman reach into his car and lift his radio microphone.

"Okay, I'll be there in a few minutes," Duncan said. The officer returned the microphone, which he hadn't turned on, to its cradle.

Duncan stepped away from the car and smiled at Adams and Milstead. The three men walked over to Rags.

Officer Duncan spoke. "Son, I have to go into town. I'll be back shortly. Now if I'm not here at this roadblock, I can't keep people from going in, can I? Lem there is going to be driving the grader into the beach area in a while. I guess there's nothing I can do if he invites you to ride with him and you think you want to. If you're real careful."

The patrolman looked at Adams and Milstead. "Well," he said, "I'm gone."

Officer Duncan winked sternly at Rags as he turned to go, and Rags grinned thankfully after him as the officer started his car and departed.

A few minutes' work by Adams and Lem saw the grader sitting on the muddy highway, ready to go.

"What we'll do, Rags," Lem said, "is not drop the blade. We'll just head for Crystal Beach, though it'll be rough going. We may have to use the blade to get through. But we should make it in an hour or so."

Rags waved to Adams as he crawled up on the big machine. "Isn't Mister Adams leaving now?" the boy asked when he observed the truck driver light a cigar and lean back against his truck.

"No," said Milstead. "Harm's gonna stay at the roadblock until Officer Duncan gets back."

Adams waved a calloused hand at the departing pair.

The grader moved easily along the highway through High Island. Although all of them were standing, it appeared that most of the buildings in the beach community had been severely damaged by the hurricane.

Below High Island, Milstead turned the grader toward Crystal Beach. Several times he was forced to drop the blade to push debris from the highway.

Fishing piers, cabins, and even an old car lay along the beach highway. Rags' heart sank. For the first time he realized what destructive force a hurricane could inflict. Their progress in the big, awkward yellow machine was much slower than the operator had predicted. It was almost two hours later before the grader came to a stop in front of the wreckage that had been Becker's Store.

"We'll walk now," Milstead said.

19

THE BRUTAL DEVASTATION numbed Rags. He surveyed what once was a service station, an ice-house, and Becker's Store. "Oh, Patches," the boy murmured aloud.

"It doesn't look good, son," the operator of the road grader said in a gruff whisper, shaking his head.

Rags saw a buzzard overhead. The scavenger was floating down in the direction of the shapeless, yellow-haired body of an animal. Rags darted toward the indistinguishable carcass. "Get away. Get away," he screamed, waving his arms at the buzzard. It flapped upward.

The boy fell only three or four yards from the decaying animal.

"That's not your dog," Milstead said. He pulled Rags to his feet. "Boy, that's a goat."

"Patches survived. He survived, Mister Milstead," the boy said between clenched teeth. "He's here. He's not dead like this goat."

Rags resumed his walk into the destroyed beach community. Debris was everywhere. Lumber from homes, an old refrigerator, half a mattress, and a bashed outdoor barbecue grill were lying in the middle of the sand-blanketed concrete highway.

The boy trotted several yards toward the beach before he was stopped by the floodwaters. He looked into the distance where the beach shack should have stood. "Nothing. There's nothing left."

The cabin had been completely demolished. The water had run down from the dunes, but Rags could see nothing remaining of the old house. Only the brightly painted pilings which had held the Taylor cabin aloft were standing. And only a few of the cabins back beyond Becker's Store remained intact.

"Lord. Lord." Rags slumped to his knees. "God, I know Patches isn't worth much when put up against all that's been ruined and washed off here," he prayed.

He remembered words his mother had taught him. He raised his arms straight out from his body, with his palms open and upward. "Holy Mary, Mother of God. Blessed is the fruit of Thy womb, Jesus." He had forgotten parts of the prayer.

"Lord, Uncle Wash said You knew what Patches had done, that You were watching over him . . ."

A gruff animal cry cut through Rags' prayer.

He leaped to his feet and looked around wildly.

Fifty yards away, walking over the rubbish of the highway was a priest attempting to hold on to a short piece of rope. His efforts were complicated by the lank, yellow-haired dog on the other end who lunged powerfully against the restraint.

Danny Ragsdale knew that dog anywhere. Patches knew that boy anywhere.

"Patches. PATCHES," screamed Rags.

Rags' feet were flying now, his arms pumping in perfect precision. He leaped over tree limbs and buckets and the crushed debris of the town.

Patches gave one mighty tug and the rope flew from the hand of the priest.

Yelps from the dog and happy cries from the boy intermingled as each raced toward the other.

They met on a pile of sand and shell left by the receding gulf waters. Patches' front legs grasped the shoulders of the kneeling boy and Rags' arms wrapped tightly around the waist of the animal as joyful tears glistened on his cheeks. Patches licked at the boy's eyes.

Milstead and the priest hurried toward the embracing pair. Lem stopped a few feet away. "Well, I'll be doggoned," he said.

"A felicitous choice of words," said the priest.

"It's Patches, Mister Milstead. It really, truly is my dog Patches."

Patches barked happily. It was really, truly his boy Rags.

20

"No one could have been more surprised than I," Father Timothy commented to Rags and Mr. Milstead.

The priest, the boy, the grader operator, and the dog sat in Father Timothy's study at the little beach parish's rectory.

"The eye of the storm passed through here about midnight Friday. It's a little late in life for me to be running from hurricanes, and I felt I might be of some use here," the old priest explained. Rags intently observed Father Timothy's weathered hands and wrinkled face as the priest punctuated his account with gestures.

"About noon Saturday, after the storm had passed, I came out of my storm cellar and was astonished at what I saw. Even though I've been through seven storms in my lifetime, I suppose I'll always be amazed at their destructiveness," Father Timothy continued.

"As you can see, the church is badly damaged and most of the roofing is gone from the rectory. But the Merciful God was kind to me in my old age. I suppose your dog and I are the only living creatures to survive the hurricane."

Rags stroked the dog at his feet, as he had done dozens of times in the past hour.

"But how did you find Patches?" he asked.

The priest smoothed his soiled black trousers and with a forefinger stretched his collar away from his neck.

"It's hard to believe," Father Timothy said wonderingly. "I started to examine the area Saturday afternoon, the day after the storm. But the water hadn't gone down enough for me to get far from the church.

"This morning, I could see the water was only partially covering the main highway, so I began walking toward the place where I met you today. I had walked almost to Becker's Store and was getting ready to walk back to the church. I was so disturbed by the destruction.

"I heard moaning. All I could see was a big barrel lodged against a gasoline pump near the store and a poor goat, obviously dead, a few feet away.

"I turned back toward the church, and that's when the moan became louder. I thought it came from within the barrel, and when I walked over, the saddest brown eyes you have ever seen looked out at me.

"It was Patches here, with a fiddle case in his mouth."

Rags smiled at his dog, and rubbed his fur again.

"I coaxed the dog out of the barrel after turning it sideways; it was standing upright against the gasoline pump," Father Timothy went on.

"I patted him and reached for the case in his mouth. Patches there was mighty weak looking, but he growled at me when I reached for the case. I tried to get him to come with me, but he wouldn't do it.

"I looked around and found a rope, tied it to his neck, and tried to lead him back to the church. He still would not come.

"Frankly, I was rather irritated with him, but I came all the way back to the church, found some dried beef in the cellar, walked back, and—with the food—got him to follow me back here. It was only when I put the beef down in front of him that he let go of the case in his mouth. After he ate, he was willing to let me inspect the case."

Father Timothy sat back and sighed. "That must be some prize fiddle you have, son."

"My fiddle really is here," said Rags wonderingly. "Patches saved it!"

The priest smiled and nodded. "So he did."

Father Timothy reached under his desk and pulled out the fiddle case. Rags took the instrument from the sturdy case and stroked it fondly. He plucked a string and was pleased with the sound.

Then Rags told of his flight from the beach with

Mr. and Mrs. Taylor and how he had discovered too late that Patches was gone. He told Father Timothy and Milstead it was clear that Patches had returned to the beach shack for the fiddle.

"You couldn't have expected him to take his job so seriously," the operator offered.

"Of course not," Father Timothy agreed. "Now, only the Lord and Patches know—but how do you think he got into that barrel?" the priest asked Rags.

Rags laughed. "That was my dining room table—a barrel with the bottom cut out. Patches just crawled inside when the storm struck."

Patches barked, and the two men laughed.

"If you could only talk, Patches," said Rags. "You'd have quite a story to tell. How about that, Patches? You and Father Timothy rode out the storm. You're a hero again."

Rags didn't realize how much fuss would be made over Patches when it was learned the dog and the priest had survived Hurricane Claudette.

Rags spent the remainder of the day and that night with Father Timothy, Milstead having to return to his road-clearing work. The boy wanted to inspect all the interesting things in the part of the rectory that wasn't damaged and to explore the storm cellar. But more, he needed a good meal, which the priest provided from canned goods and bottled water stored in the storm cellar.

The next morning, Father Timothy, Patches, and Rags were inspecting the storm's damage when Rags heard what sounded like an airplane. He looked into the bright sky, for it was a beautifully clear day, to see a helicopter circling a few hundred yards away.

By the time the aircraft landed, Father Timothy, Rags, and Patches were close enough to see "CBC News" written on the side of the machine.

"Planes and helicopters have been flying around here for a couple of days," the priest observed. "I could tell they were taking photographs of the damage. But this is the first one to land."

The helicopter landed in the middle of the highway, where Milstead's grader, joined by two others now, had cleared away debris only a short time before.

Lem walked over to the priest and Rags, shaking his head. "I'm afraid I let it out, Father, that you and this dog here survived the hurricane. I told my boss last night about you and the dog and this boy here. This morning I guess he notified the press and radio and TV people. He said he was driving some newspaper reporters down this morning and that other press people would probably be in the area today."

"That's okay, Lem," Father Timothy smiled. "The Lord can use some good publicity. You know —He moves in mysterious ways."

Within minutes, the priest and the boy were being interviewed by the television crew that arrived in the helicopter. A cameraman shot several minutes of film while Rags and Father Timothy answered the questions for the network news.

During the next two hours, many more news people appeared on the beach. Father Timothy and

Rags told their stories over and over. A great many pictures were taken, mostly of the insistent Patches. Rags remarked that his partner hadn't lost his taste for an audience.

With the coming of the news representatives, the beach area came to life. By early afternoon, electrical workers were on the scene restoring service to the town.

At midafternoon, Rags was exhausted. But his weariness fell away when he saw a familiar face approaching. It was that of Tucker LaFleur.

Rags didn't care much for a public display of affection and neither did Tucker LaFleur. The big shrimper ruffled Rags' auburn hair and bent over to rub the golden fur of Patches. The dog licked his hand in recognition.

"I heard about you on the noon news," LaFleur told Rags. "That is some story. You and this dog are quite a pair. Back in Port Arthur, you're famous. I heard the mayor say on the radio that the whole city should be proud of you, havin' won the talent contest and all at the Cajun Festival. Maybe your daddy has heard and will be looking for you."

Rags jumped at the thought.

"Guess I should be getting home, huh, Mister LaFleur?" Rags wondered aloud.

"Pro'bly so, son," the shrimper replied.

"C'mon, I'll take you back," he added.

Rags said goodbye to the priest. "I thank you for your kindness," he said.

"This reunion has been thanks enough," replied the priest. "God goes with you, my son." Father

Timothy bent over to stroke Patches. "And apparently with you, too, Brother Patches," he laughed.

Rags and Tucker joined in, and Patches barked as if he understood perfectly.

Father Timothy moved away.

"Goodbye, Father," Rags called.

The old priest waved and walked toward his church.

As Rags and Patches climbed into Tucker La-Fleur's Jeep, a photographer called, "Just one more, hugging the dog, please."

That was a request Rags was happy to oblige.

21

RAGS RODE UP FRONT with Tucker, and Patches sat behind in the open Jeep.

"You done a lot of growin' up since I saw you last," LaFleur said to Rags. "Evangeline will be happy to see you."

The mention of the large Cajun woman brought a smile from Rags. "I'll be happy to see her, too," he said.

LaFleur returned the subject to Rags' father. "Rags, Evangeline and I have been asking around about your daddy. You haven't had any word on him, have you?"

Rags said he had not.

"Well, we'll just have to keep looking. Maybe the news of you and Patches and this hurricane will reach your papa and he'll come for you," LaFleur offered. "Why don't you show me your house. Maybe he's gone back to check the damage."

Rags agreed it was worth a try.

"I've got a feeling, Rags, the mayor's gonna try to put some kind of medal on Patches. You, too, maybe," LaFleur said. "The mayor's not gonna let a good shot at this kind of publicity for his city go by without makin' some points. You and that dog are national news."

"We haven't done anything," Rags said. "Especially not me. Patches is a hero, if there is one. And Father Timothy."

"Yeah," said LaFleur, "but you're the one the mayor can stand up in front of city hall and point to as the kind of young American we can all be proud of. The kind that sets a goal, like your settin' out to find Patches and not stoppin' till you found him. Positive thinking, you know?" LaFleur went on. "The mayor will point out that we all need to be positive thinkers like my young fran' and fella citizen Daniel Ragsdale here. That's what that Mayor Parkhouse's goin' to say," said LaFleur with a grand sweep of his arms.

Rags chuckled, then grew serious.

"Well, I just wish I could find my pa," he sighed.

Two hours later, LaFleur drove through Port Arthur and onto Rainbow Bridge. "Quite a sight from up here, huh, Rags?" LaFleur asked. "We'll be at your house in no time now, if the water doesn't keep us out."

But the water did. Rags could tell from atop Rainbow Bridge that the area where he had lived was flooded. LaFleur pulled off the main highway a few minutes later. The Jeep jerked onto the road which led to Rags' home.

Four hundred yards down the road, high water forced LaFleur to stop. "There's no gettin' in there, Rags. Your pa can't have got in either. We won't find him this time."

Rags frowned. "Uncle Wash's cabin, if it's still there, is flooded, too. And the place Patches and I lived. I didn't realize there would be this much water. How long will it take for the water to go down?" he asked LaFleur.

"I don' know. A week, maybe."

LaFleur turned the Jeep around.

"You're welcome to come stay with me till you decide what to do. Or Evangeline will be tickled to have you," LaFleur offered.

"Staying with you sounds fine," Rags said. "But I sure want to find Pa, now. It's been a good while. We spent some mighty happy days down here, and I figure we can again. I just feel like Pa's all right after all this time. I figured he was the day he hit that Wilson, 'cept I guess he didn't know it then."

"You're growin' up more than I thought," the shrimper said. "You come on with me. Things'll work out."

The trip back across Rainbow Bridge to the docks in Port Arthur took little time. Patches bounded from the Jeep in front of Evangeline's cafe before LaFleur could bring the vehicle to a halt.

Patches' barks brought Evangeline rushing outside.

"*Mon cher,*" she cried as she threw open her arms and hugged Rags. "*Mon cher, mon Rags,*" she

repeated over and over. She finally looked up at La-
Fleur—who was humming a tune, a little impa-
tiently, to himself, and seemed to be studying a
cloud.

Evangeline hurried the man, the boy, and dog
into the cafe and in quick order had cold shrimp,
crab and raw oysters before them. Patches was busy
on the floor gnawing a large bone.

Evangeline fussed about, shooing flies from the
table and filling the diners' bowls with more red
sauce. She drew a cold beer for LaFleur and poured
Rags iced tea from a big glass pitcher.

"Rags, *mon cher,* you have been on that television aw'ready. And that dog there. He gon' be a
movie star for sure," Evangeline crowed.

She left the table to wait on the gathering crowd
at the bar.

LaFleur addressed Rags. "Why don't you and
Patches go out with me on the shrimp boat tomor-
row. I haven't been out since before the hurricane.
Should be good trawlin' now."

Rags gladly accepted.

"That will give you time to decide what you
want to do about starting out again to find your pa,"
LaFleur commented.

Evangeline was returning to the table with another beer for LaFleur. She heard him mention Rags'
father.

The woman sat down, leaning her arms on the
table. She cupped her hands together. LaFleur knew
from years of watching Evangeline that she had
something serious to say.

"When all this news start today 'bout you and

that man of God and your Patches, there was all kinds of talk in here about who you belonged to, Rags," Evangeline began.

Nodding toward LaFleur, Evangeline said, "You know, *mon cher,* when we saw Rags and Patches on the noon TV news and you said you were goin' to the beach to get our Rags—some fellas here heard you say that. They asked me after you left if that boy and dog on television are not the ones they heard about who were here a while back. I told them that, yeah, that is the truth. And that this Rags, he is looking for his father, yeah.

"Anyhow, a man at the bar said that if he is Roland Ragsdale's boy, then the boy goin' to have to go to the Rio Grande Valley to find him. He signed on a barge crew headed for Brownsville—this man was on the crew with him. The fella, he say Rags' papa decided to stay in that Gran' Rio Valley to harvest crops and make some more money before he come back to get Rags."

Rags asked Evangeline for a map so he could see where the Rio Grande Valley and Brownsville were located. She produced one from under the counter.

"There it is," LaFleur said, pointing to the map. "That's Brownsville, and all along here," he traced a finger across the map, "is the Rio Grande Valley. They grow lots of vegetables and fruit down there."

Rags stared at the map for a long while before handing it back to Evangeline.

Next morning found Rags, Patches, and La-Fleur running the shrimp boat across a calm, open sea. Seagulls followed in their wake, hurling themselves into the water above the nets to scavenge shrimp.

The catch was good. Rags could see LaFleur was pleased as they drew into the shrimp dock late that afternoon. Once the shrimp were unloaded onto the conveyer at the shrimp house, LaFleur was ready to head for Evangeline's.

"Aren't you going to wait and get your money?" Rags asked.

"No," said LaFleur. "I can tell you to a half pound how much I have, and they know I know it," he said, pointing a thumb over his shoulder toward Colonel McDaniel's shrimp house.

As they entered the cafe, Evangeline rushed to LaFleur with a newspaper in each hand. She hugged Rags and LaFleur in one sweep, then reached down to stroke Patches, who raised up on his back legs to paw affectionately at Evangeline's stomach.

She pushed the boy and man to the table in the corner. Rags felt it had now become their own personal table. Patches flopped to the floor under the table, drained of his energy after the day on the shrimp boat. Rags was tired but happy.

"Should have seen our catch," he told Evangeline.

"Later, later, *mon cher*. I have news," she interrupted.

She showed them a story in the morning newspaper which said Rags was motherless and that the whereabouts of Rags' father were unknown. The story recited how Rags had been alone for several weeks, wandering in search of his father. The story quoted a Mr. and Mrs. Taylor and related the events of recent days during and after the hurricane.

Evangeline then spread on the table a second newspaper.

"This is the afternoon paper and look what it say."

LaFleur read the story, which repeated that Rags "was alone in the world" and quoted one county official as saying that Rags should be made a ward of the state.

"What does that mean, a ward of the state?" Rags asked.

Evangeline said she too had asked that question and a customer said that meant there would be a hearing before a judge, and that the judge would decide what should be done with Rags. Evangeline said she was told Rags would probably be placed in a foster home until it could be decided where he would ultimately live.

"But I don't need a home," Rags frowned, "I have you and Tucker when I need a home. I've got to keep looking for my pa. I can't do that in some . . . what did you call it?"

"Foster home," LaFleur said.

"Yeah, foster home," Rags repeated.

LaFleur, Evangeline, and Rags grew quiet, individually studying the situation. Then Evangeline spoke softly:

"They know you are here, Rags. A sheriff's deputy came by and said they knew you left the beach with Tucker and that you had been here. I told them you were on the boat with Tucker. That you would be here tonight." Her head slumped forward as she spoke.

She looked at LaFleur, tears growing in her eyes. "I wouldn't have told them if I know it would . . ." she sobbed, her voice decreasing to a whisper.

LaFleur patted her hand. "You did the right thing, Vangy," he quietly said.

LaFleur looked at Rags. "Tomorrow we'll get you cleaned up good and take you to the law. They'll do what's right. I'll ask them if you can stay with me, if that's what you want."

Rags, confused, nodded his head affirmatively.

LaFleur continued, "I have friends who will vouch for me that you would be okay with me. You'll stay with me."

Evangeline insisted LaFleur bring Rags' clothes to her later in the evening, that she would wash them. "He must look his best tomorrow," she fussed.

The boy slept fitfully that night despite the comfort of LaFleur's neat cottage. Patches, aware of his master's uneasiness, eased to Rags' side and nudged his arm.

Moonlight streaked through the cottage's windows as Rags wrapped an arm around the dog's neck. "If it wasn't for Evangeline and Tucker, we'd leave here tonight," Rags said.

Patches whined in agreement.

The Rio Grande Valley, Rags thought as he finally drifted into sleep, seemed a very long way off.

22

A LARGE CLOCK ON THE WALL of the sheriff's office showed nine o'clock as Rags and LaFleur entered through a swinging door. LaFleur removed his cap.

Rags ran a hand over the bib of his overalls. "Evangeline did a good job on my clothes, didn't she?" he asked the big shrimper. The sneakers had been washed and his overalls and the shirt he had been given at the farmhouse were washed, starched, and ironed. Rags' auburn hair had been combed back, but strands still fell to his forehead.

As the boy and LaFleur neared the desk of a man wearing a badge over his left shirt pocket, Rags unknowingly slipped nearer LaFleur's side.

"I'm here with Danny Ragsdale," LaFleur said to the man, who immediately jumped from his chair, recognizing Rags.

"So this is the boy who has the famous dog," the man said. "I'm Deputy Griffin." He shook hands with LaFleur and Rags.

"You're some type of hero around here," Griffin said. "Been reading all about you."

"I called last night," LaFleur said. "They told me to bring Rags in this morning."

"Yeah," Griffin said, absently thumbing some papers on his desk. He appeared embarrassed to be involved in Rags' case. "You're supposed to go up-stairs to Judge Wilkerson's office. He's waiting there for you."

LaFleur thanked the deputy, then led Rags to an elevator. They rode to an upper floor and even-tually arrived in front of a door marked, "Judge Wilkerson." A thin woman greeted them inside and led them through another door, where she an-nounced, "Mister LaFleur and Danny Ragsdale to see you, Your Honor."

Behind a huge desk sat an elderly man with half-moon glasses, behind which sparkled two kind eyes. He rose as they entered. Rags had never before seen such silver hair. The flowing locks hung almost to the man's shoulders.

Judge Wilkerson was taller than LaFleur. "Good to see you, Tucker," he said, offering the shrimper his hand.

"And this must be Rags. How come you didn't bring Patches?" Judge Wilkerson laughed. He liter-ally shook when he laughed. Rags liked him right away.

"Sit down. Sit down," he waved. The judge returned to his large chair behind the mammoth desk. Rags sank into a sofa in the corner.

Judge Wilkerson picked up a long, unlighted cigar and placed it in his mouth. He studied Rags before removing the cigar and balancing it on an ashtray on the desk.

"Young man, you've made quite a stir in these parts. Won the talent contest, you and that dog, at the festival. Your dog survives the worst hurricane we've had in years, and you run all over the country to get the dog back."

The judge leaned back in the chair, closing his eyes for a moment.

He leaned forward quickly and pointed a finger at Rags. The boy flinched.

"I like that, young man. Yes, sir, I like your style.

"I had a mother that told me, God rest her soul, she told me 'Inscribe new memories and wash away the grit.' I'd say you've inscribed some great memories around here.

"Now look, son. All that publicity you got has brought out the fact you don't have anybody. The law says I must find you a home." Judge Wilkerson paused again. It appeared to Rags the judge was staring over Rags' head at something on the wall behind him. Rags was tempted to turn around to examine whatever it was. The judge looked back at Rags, at Tucker LaFleur, then back at the boy.

"What do you think about being in a foster home, son?" the judge asked. "You need a roof over your head, you know."

Rags tried to swallow the lump in his throat. "I . . . I . . ." Rags remembered the secretary addressing the judge as "Your Honor."

"Your Honor, sir, judge," Rags began. Judge Wilkerson subdued a smile. "I have a roof over my head, Your Honor."

"But you need companions," the judge interjected.

"I have companions, sir," the boy replied.

"But Rags, you need good friends to watch out for you," the judge insisted, "to help and guide you."

Rags looked directly at the judge. "Your Honor, I have Patches. He's the best friend in the world, and he'll help me find my pa."

Rags realized what he had said and blushed. He looked at Tucker, who smiled back. "And Mister LaFleur and Evangeline. They're my friends," Rags said.

Judge Wilkerson rocked back in his chair. "Rags, I agree with all you say. But I have to make a decision. Why don't you please excuse Mister La-Fleur and me for a minute. You can wait outside in my secretary's office. Better yet, want to see the courtroom?"

Rags said he did. The judge escorted Rags to a side door of the office, opened it, and guided the boy to a large chair placed on a platform about three feet above the floor of the courtroom.

Judge Wilkerson pulled the chair around, then placed his hand on a desk built into the platform. "This is what we call the 'bench.' It's from here I listen to the cases that come before me. You try the chair on for size while I talk to Tucker."

Rags climbed into the chair. Judge Wilkerson walked back to the office, chuckling. As soon as the judge closed the door, Rags looked out over the courtroom, remembering a trial his class in school had conducted. Rags announced, "The court is now in session. Please be seated."

Inside the private office of Judge Wilkerson, Tucker LaFleur stood as the judge returned. "Sit down, Tucker, sit down," the judge instructed. Judge Wilkerson chose the couch Rags had vacated, within arm's length of LaFleur.

"Okay, Tucker. We've been friends for a long time. You helped me in my first campaign. You really brought in the Cajun vote that time." Judge Wilkerson chuckled, remembering that first campaign so many years ago.

"How do you stay so young, Tucker? You don't look a bit older now than then." The judge closed his eyes a moment, then opened them and stood. "But first things first," the judge said.

"Tucker, tell me what you think." LaFleur started to speak, but the judge spoke first. "I'm thinking of letting you have him, Tucker. But you tell me what's on your mind."

LaFleur studied the judge. "Judge," he began, "you've always been a people's judge. I guess you can't grow up on the streets here and not be. You brought fairness to the courthouse. You've been honest with me and the people, and I want to be honest with you." LaFleur hesitated before continuing.

"Judge, Rags isn't going to stay no matter where you put him. He's got it dead set in his head to go find his papa," LaFleur explained. He told the judge of the latest report on Rags' father.

The magistrate rubbed his chin.

"Tucker," he said. "Did you know I ran away from home when I was fourteen?" He didn't wait for an answer. "I stayed gone a year. I hired out on a boat. Saw lots of world. I think that experience made me a better man. And I know it helped me in my decisions as a judge."

Judge Wilkerson reflected. "That year on the boat made me self-sufficient. I remember how people wanted to stand in my way. 'Course, some of 'em knew what they were talking about. It wasn't easy."

LaFleur nodded pensively.

"That boy will make it, though, Tucker. I agree with you. He won't stay where we put him anyway."

Judge Wilkerson turned to LaFleur. "Tucker, I'm going to authorize you as a foster parent. I'm going to put Danny Ragsdale in your care. Like you say, he'll head out looking for his father. You and I know that. Others don't have to know. Keep me posted, Tucker." LaFleur recognized the last sentence as a dismissal.

"Thank you, judge. I'll let you know what happens."

LaFleur shook hands with Judge Wilkerson, then walked into the courtroom. Rags was pointing at an imaginary plaintiff before the bench. LaFleur walked around in front of Rags and looked up at the boy acting the part of a judge. "Rags, the judge says you can stay with me." Rags smiled in relief and joined his friend on the floor of the courtroom.

Patches leaped on Rags as the boy entered the door of LaFleur's cottage. "We don't have to go to any old foster home," Rags told the dog. "We're gonna stay with Tucker."

That evening, though, Rags asked the shrimper if he could again see a map of Texas. LaFleur found one, saying nothing as he handed the map over. LaFleur reached down to playfully tap Patches under the chin. Then he ruffled Rags' hair before moving quietly toward his room.

"Tucker . . ." Rags called hesitantly. LaFleur turned. He knew the boy's thoughts. He would have loved for Rags and Patches to stay with him forever. But he knew Rags would be happy only when he found his father.

Rags started to speak again. LaFleur looked at him and said simply, "It's okay, Rags. Get a good night's sleep."

Later Rags and Patches lay on the bed in the room LaFleur had provided for them. A huge moon glimmered over the bay. Rags circled an arm around the dog. "Patches, I figure if we leave tonight, with luck we'll be in Brownsville by the weekend."

The boy rose from the bed and, moving quietly as possible, slipped on his overalls. He stroked Patches, then reached for the fiddle case on a nearby chair. He opened the case and put the Texas map inside.

Rags motioned to Patches to follow him as he silently moved to the front door. The boy eased the door open and waved Patches ahead. He quickly followed the dog outside.

Tucker LaFleur lay back on his bed, his hands linked behind his head. He heard the faint closing of the door. The shrimper turned on his side to look out the window near his bed. He watched the silhouettes of the boy and the dog race across the yard and disappear into the night.

LaFleur smiled and pulled the sheet over his shoulders.

As he closed his eyes, he sighed and softly murmured, "So long Rags. So long Patches."

His only answer was the whisper of a breeze that had completed a sea passage of thousands of miles to stir the curtain near his head.